The Burying Beetle

The Burying Beetle

ANN KELLEY

Luath Press Limited

EDINBURGH

www.luath.co.uk

Material from *The Badger* by Ernest Neal reprinted by permission
of HarperCollins Ltd © 1969 Ernest Neal.

Extract from 'Sunday Night' from *All of Us: The Collected Poems* by
Raymond Carver, published by Harvill Press © Tess Gallagher.
Reproduced by permission of The Random House Group Ltd and ICM.

'The Summer Day' from *House of Light* by Mary Oliver.
Copyright © 1990 by Mary Oliver.
Reprinted by permission of Beacon Press, Boston.

Extract from 'This be the Verse' from *Collected Poems*
by Philip Larkin reproduced by permission of
Faber and Faber Ltd © 2003 and Farrar, Straus & Giroux Inc © 2004.

First published 2005

The paper used in this book is recyclable.
It is made from low-chlorine pulps produced in a low-energy,
low-emission manner from renewable forests.

The publisher acknowledges subsidy from the Scottish Arts Council

Scottish
Arts Council

towards the publication of this volume.

Printed and bound by
Creative Print and Design, Ebbw Vale

Typeset in 10.5 point Sabon
by Jennie Renton

*For Chloe, Flora, Sam, Caroline and Mark,
and in memory of Nathan.*

Acknowledgements

Thank you all friends and family members who read early drafts of *The Burying Beetle*: Robert, Lily, Ann, Gaynor, Carolyn, Caroline, Ron, Mark, Helen, Michael B, Michael F, Marion, Jenny Strong, Alan Bleakely and Simon Butler.

Thank you Roger Phillips for checking my nature facts, and a special thank you to Year 10 of St Ives School who kindly allowed me to read it to them during their lunch breaks and made such useful comments.

A big thank you to all at Luath – a great small press – kind, helpful, encouraging, very hard working, and my editor Jennie Renton, whose patience over the phone was little short of miraculous.

IT WAS AFTER I ate King that everything started to go wrong in our entire family, as if someone had put an evil spell onto us, a hex – like a bad fairy godmother had said at my birth, 'When you are eleven you are going to be struck by a sorrow so big it will be like a lightning bolt. There will be grief like a sharp rock in your throat.'

CHAPTER ONE

Silphidae – Necrophorus vespillo
The Burying Beetle has the curious habit of burying dead
birds, mice, shrews, voles and other animals by digging the
earth away beneath them. This accomplished, the beetle
deposits her eggs upon the dead carcase, and when the larvae,
or grubs, hatch they find an abundant food-supply near at
hand. These insect-scavengers perform useful work, and it's
largely because of their efforts that so few corpses of wild
creatures are discovered. These carrion beetles also devour
some of the decomposing flesh of the carcase, seeming to
relish the bad odour that is given off. The Burying Beetle is
rarely seen, unless close watch is kept over a dead rodent,
bird, or other animal, and they seem to fly about on their
scavenging expeditions in pairs, being attracted to the spot
by scent. The commonest species is brownish black with
bands and spots of orange-yellow.

British Insects by W. Percival Westell, FLS

(The Abbey Nature Books)

NOW, WHEN I throw out a dead mouse, I shall note where the body lands, watch for a pair of winged gravediggers to arrive and inhale as if they have just arrived at the seaside. I'll watch them tuck in to a morsel of meat, have sex on the putrefying flesh, then bury the evidence. Weird, or what!

Today, the eleventh day of August 1999, is my twelfth birthday.

The sun didn't rise this morning, or if it did it was so cloaked in dark grey cloud that the sky barely lightened. And then it rained. Not the sort of rain that looks like long knives, but a very Cornish drizzle – a sea mist, a mizzle that soaks you through just as thoroughly as a downpour.

We're staying in this cottage on the edge of a cliff overlooking a long white beach. Today, it's as if the cottage is in the sky on its own island of dull green, the tall pines hung with glistening cobwebs as if summer has gone and suddenly it's autumn. Like that feeling you get when it's time to go back to school after a long hot summer, and you put on your winter uniform for the first time, and can't remember how to tie the stupid tie, and you remember getting up in the dark, and going home in the dark. I hate that. The thought of a long dark winter ahead. But I do quite like the feeling of the season changing; my school beret snug on my head; knee-socks; lace-up shoes; the warm smell of my own breath under the striped woollen scarf.

Today, no birds come to the feeder hanging from the copper beech.

There's no sound of sea, even. A heavy grey blanket muffles the waves' collapsing sound on the sand. Ghost gulls moan and whine. There's not a hope in hell of seeing the eclipse, even though Totality is immediately over this part of Cornwall. But at 10.30am we put on waterproofs and walk through the gate onto the coast path. We push through sodden bracken, our shoes and jeans' hems soaked immediately, and walk to the railway bridge. All along the coast path there are little groups of people. A man with a small child on his shoulder. A family huddled under a golf umbrella. The sky a solid grey. No light bits, no fluffy bits or streaky bits, just a dead greyness, heavy with moisture. It's like being in the middle of a cloud. We *are* in the middle of a cloud.

People line the path at the highest point where there's a panoramic view of the bay and its beaches. Even the beach below us is crowded with people. Not loaded down with buckets and spades, ice creams, windbreaks, and with gritty sand in their private parts, but carrying umbrellas and wearing wellies and waterproofs. And we have all come together to share this moment. And just before 11am, as promised, we can see an even darker darkness spreading from the west over towards Clodgy, coming towards us, enveloping us in a cold clamminess. The gulls are silent.

And at the Moment of Totality, cameras flash on every beach on this side of the bay – Carbis, Porthminster, the Island, and over towards Newquay, Gwithian, Phillack, and Hayle. The sky is dark and all the bright stars have fallen and are twinkling among us.

Brilliant! Today at this very minute, I am twelve, and I feel in my bones that something momentous will happen to me. (Anyway, being eleven was so shitty, it's got to be better this year.)

'Jack! You are aware it's your Daughter's Birthday? No card or present! You could at least Phone her.' Mum slams down the phone. 'Where is he, Damn him?'

'Mum?'

'Sorry Sweetie, I just thought I'd try your father. He's Not There.'

'Oh!' I try to look disappointed. Mum thinks I must be upset that Daddy didn't remember my birthday. I forgive him. He's got some good reason, I'm sure. Men aren't any good at stuff like birthdays and anniversaries. I read somewhere that it's because they have more important things to think about, like earning money and fighting wars – or anyway, they think they're more important things. I think the female of the species have far more important things to think about – like looking after their babies and caring for their families, cooking healthy food for them and hugging them a lot.

Perhaps there'll be a second post.

I hated it when we first came here. There's a farm above us on the top of the hill and you could hear the cows calling for their calves all day long. I know they have to take them away from the mothers so the cows will carry on producing milk for people, but it's so cruel. I don't drink cow's milk and I don't think many people would if they only knew how cruel it is to produce the stuff. Soys don't have babies.

The countryside is so much scarier than the city. It's all life or death here.

Our townie cats have practically gone wild. They spend all day hunting and bring in half dead creatures – voles, which they don't even eat, just leave them on the floor for us to tread on. Harvest mice – which are so pretty – golden honey coloured with the longest whiskers – are carried in and let go, so the three cats have sport all day, trying to recapture the terrified little things. They work together, like a pack of lions or a pride or whatever. They take turns – one keeps guard while the others sleep.

We even get slow-worms, which are grey-pink, with a silvery stripe. Sometimes the cats chew them a bit and let them go. I have decided that slow-worms are the best thing about living

6

here. They suddenly appear on the floor in the sitting room and the cats are a little scared of them. It's the fear of serpents thingy, I expect. Inbuilt sensible fears that keep you from being stung or poisoned or bitten.

I'm not frightened to pick slow-worms up, though I read in one of the trillion books here (I love books) that they can bite. But their jaws are so tiny that they couldn't manage anything but a nip anyway. They feel very cool and not slippery or slimy at all, just cool and smooth. But they don't like to be handled, they squirm like mad, so I usually just throw them out into the garden and hope the cats don't see where they've gone.

It's a bit like a zoo in this house. Apart from the slow-worms and mice and voles, we have crickets. There's a plague of them at the moment, on the curtains, on the wooden ceiling, leaping around the carpet and confounding (I think that's the word) the cats' attempts to catch them.

I never saw a cricket in London. Though of course I've seen and heard cicadas in hot countries, when Mum used to take me away each winter. That was the good side of being a Sickly Child. Getting out of school and cold wet winters to go somewhere warm and sunny and just swim and snorkel and lie around all day reading. Heaven!

I remember a very sad looking praying mantis that was trying to climb a wall and he only had one back leg. I should think it makes you totally confused losing one of your jumping legs. I like praying mantises. I had one once in Kenya – I rescued it from the loo. It was nearly drowned but had kept its head above water. I fished it out and put it to dry on a piece of toilet paper on the table next to my bed. It was fine, and it stayed there for ages, just watching me. I could feel its huge eyes following me around the room, like Mona Lisa's. It was the most beautiful bright apple green and had an articulated neck and head. Like a large truck. It stayed three days. It must have been grateful and was trying to tell me.

Our house is ramshackle – I love that word – it sounds just like it is – a sort of black-painted shack on the edge of a cliff. And there's a big beach below us. I can walk down across the rocks, but I have to take ages getting up again. Keep stopping for breath. But that's OK. There's no one to see me struggling, except Mum.

That's the main problem of being here. There's no one around.

When Mum said we were moving out of London for my health and coming to St Ives, I thought we would be in the middle of the old town and I could sit on Porthmeor Beach and watch the sun set, and be able to make friends. It's always been a dream of mine to live here, ever since we came a few years ago, when Mum and Daddy were happy together. It's sort of idyllic and I just love everything about it: the gulls everywhere, their calling to each other, the surfers riding the big waves, the little boats bobbing in the harbour, the artists' studios we looked round, the white sand that almost blinds you when you look at it without sunglasses on.

'Sweetie – will you answer the door…?

'… I'm in the bathroom.' I finish the sentence for her.

'Miss Gussie Stevens?'

'Yes, that's me!' This very wet looking (I mean soaked wet) man has a huge cellophane-wrapped bouquet in his big red hands.

'Birthday, is it?'

'Yes, how did you know?'

'Lovely view you've got here!'

'Yes, thanks!'

The flowers – all red and yellow carnations and purple irises – from Daddy, of course.

Happy Birthday, Babe! All my love – Daddy xxx

'Hmm! Typical!' Mum fumes when she gets out of the bathroom.

Well I think they're wonderful. I sniff them, but there's no scent at all. It's a very grown-up sort of present. No one's ever given me flowers, except in hospital.

I stick them all over the house. In my room mostly, so I can appreciate them, but I've left a few in the sitting room too. I put all the red carnations together, cut short, all the yellow ones in a blue jug, and all the irises – not my favourite flower – cut down very short so the heads are mixed together and clustered, in a small white bowl on the dining table. The flowers suddenly look much nicer than they had in the bouquet, all tall and precious and posh looking. I throw out the nasty ferny stuff, much too weddingy. Now they look like mine, from my own darling Daddy.

'God what a Dreadful Day, so Dark and Gloomy.' Mum hates it when the weather keeps her in. She sounds like Eeyore. The rain's coming down in buckets now and we need buckets to catch the drips that come in all over the house, mostly in the porch, but also in the dining room. The cats – Flaubert, Rimbaud (named by Mum and Daddy, but I call them Flo and Rambo), and Charlie, (I was allowed to name that one, I had her for my tenth birthday and she's all mine), are curled up on the small sofa, not touching each other. They occasionally open an eye, listen to the rain hammering on the roof, look thoroughly disgruntled, yawn at each other and go back to sleep. They all agree with Mum it's too wet even for hunting.

Mum has custody of me and the cats.

What are they for, anyway, yawns? I have a theory that it's a way of showing other animals (or humans) that we are not aggressive towards them. Like lions when they are about to go to sleep, they all sit around and yawn at each other. It means – I'm not going to fight you or kill you or eat you, because I'm sleepy and friendly – Aah Aah, and the other animals answer with a similar signal. Yes, I reckon that's it. I wonder if anyone has ever done any experiments on yawning. (Just thinking about yawning makes me yawn.)

For my birthday treat, (apart from the spectacular natural display God tried to put on for me, though actually it's the camera flashlights I'll remember, not the cloud-hidden eclipse), I'm having takeaway Indian food and a video. We are watching *Born Yesterday*, one of my favourite films, except I also love *It's a Wonderful Life*, but we watch that at Christmas, and that film with Marilyn Monroe, Tony Curtis and Jack someone or other – where she has these amazing dresses she's almost wearing and Tony and Jack dress up as women in an all women's band. It's so funny. Lemon! That's his name.

Daddy is the curator of the London Film Archive. He used to be a photographer and he's a film-maker too, but he does the other thing to make a living until he gets a break in the movie business. We get to see any movies we want, it's cool. Daddy gave me his old Nikkormat. It's a manual SLR camera. That means single lens reflex and it takes 35mm film. It's heavy and battered and I love it.

I also like Indiana Jones movies – I liked the first one best – *Indiana Jones and the Raiders of the Lost Ark*. I have this cool hat, which Grandpop gave me – my Grandpop, who died. It's just like Indiana Jones' hat, a sort of soft-brimmed – trilby, Grandpop called it – in a dark brown felt. He gave it to me when I was a cowboy, and he also made me a gun out of a piece of wood, carved it into a gun shape. I wore it tucked into my belt. Mum didn't approve – I'm not sure if she didn't approve of me being a cowboy or of me having a gun. Both, probably. I now wear the hat most of the time, to remind me of Grandpop and because Indy is my hero. Harrison Ford – he's so cool, even if he is rather old. I loved it when one of his students had I LOVE YOU written on her eyelids and she kept closing her eyes so he could read the message. If I ever make a movie, it has got to be like Indiana Jones movies. The woman who was Willie in *Indiana Jones and the Temple of Doom* is married to Steven Spielberg. She is just about the prettiest woman I have ever seen. It must be interesting to look like that – blonde wavy hair and big blue eyes and a wide mouth. You could have anything in the world if you looked like that.

The young Indy was played by River Phoenix – my favourite film actor of all time. He also played Chris in *Stand By Me*, which I saw when I was ten. But he died when I was three. I remember what Gordie said to Chris when he was feeling very sorry for himself – he said, 'You can be anything you want, man.'

I don't only like old or dead film stars. I like Brad Pitt and Keanu Reeves but I don't like the one who looks like a baby doll – the one with the Italian name… ?

I love the music in the Indiana Jones movies – *Da da, da di da di da di da!*

I don't have friends here yet. My best friend in London is Summer Strong. (One of River Phoenix's sisters is called Summer. How's that for a coincidence?) We got to be friends because we sat next to each other at school, and stayed together all through, and she's going to come and stay sometime during these hols. I'm so looking forward to it. I can't wait.

It's such a cool house this. It's all made of wood, even the roof, and it's painted black on the outside and white inside. There are two bedrooms upstairs and a sitting room with a tiny kitchen –

like on a yacht – and then there's a trapdoor and a stepladder to another long room downstairs. The garden is practically vertical down to the beach. There are bamboos and palms and when the sun shines the sea is a beautiful pale turquoise colour in shallow water, like it was in Kenya, and deep blue where it gets deep. It's quite exotic really. A bit of a change from Camden Town.

I forgot to mention the big trees – pines or something, absolutely huge, a line of them like an overgrown hedge on the edge of the cliff. We can't see much of the beach through the branches, but they are Good Windbreaks, Mum says. From downstairs you can see beach and sea between the huge trunks. It's like peeping through the legs of an elephant, massive, dark grey wrinkled hulks. There's a wooden deck, too, with a high rail around, but I haven't had the courage to go out there yet. I'm no good at heights.

I don't know who the owner of the house is, but whoever it is, is a great reader. There are books everywhere. They are very old and dusty, not like mine, but our books are all in store. Mum hasn't enough room for her clothes because of all the books. She is threatening to stuff them in the shed, so she can hang up her huge collection of clothes. Not that she's ever going to wear any of that stuff here. I can't imagine why she bothers. There's not exactly a flourishing social scene of the sort that she had in London. But she's OK really, apart from her intense vanity and the way she has of turning into Cruella de Vil every time she speaks to Daddy. I suppose she's had lots to put up with – not being able to go to work because of looking after me.

I don't know why she and Daddy split – it was last year, before Grandpop and Grandma died. I was in hospital some of the time anyway but when I was at home there were lots of muffled angry voices and Mum cried a lot. I suppose he was having an affair.

He lives with a woman called Eloise, which is a lovely name. I think I might change my name by deed pole... or is it poll? You can do that to make it legal. Augusta is so ugly and I get called Custard sometimes. Summer calls me Org. Daddy calls me Gussie, which is OK. Grandpop called me Princess Augusta for a while. I thought I was a real princess until I was about seven or eight. I was quite relieved when I found out I wasn't. I thought I'd have to leave home and go and live in the palace with the Queen and the Duke of Edinburgh.

I want to be known as Kezia – I'm not sure how that's pronounced. I read it in a short story by Katherine Mansfield. There's this family in a house on a bay and the women all just about tolerate the father but can't wait to get him off to work, so they can relax and enjoy themselves. There's a wonderful granny in the story who cooks and looks after the little children. I think the mother is sickly, or she's just had a baby or something. She's a wuss; the father is stuffy and demanding and the women all run round looking after him. It doesn't sound much but it's a lovely story. It makes me feel warm and safe for some reason. A bit like how I feel when I watch *It's a Wonderful Life*. I found it here, the book.

This house is called Peregrine, which I thought was a posh boy's name from out of a PG Wodehouse story, but which is in fact a bird of prey, but we haven't seen any yet. Not that I'd know one if I fell over it, or it hit me in the belly with a wet fish. There are loads of bird books here but I haven't got round to them yet.

Some Like it Hot! That's the name of the Marilyn Monroe film. That makes me feel warm in a different way. I love it that Mum and I laugh out loud at the same bits each time, like at the very end when Tony Curtis gets a proposal of marriage from the millionaire, and tells him he's really a man, and the millionaire says – 'Nobody's perfect!'

My favourite bit in *Born Yesterday* is when the bully shouts to the woman, 'Billie!' and she shouts back 'Whaddyawaan?' And the bit where he says, 'All this trouble just 'cos a broad reads a book!' I so love her voice. It's all small and squeaky except when she's yelling 'Whaddyawaan?' And the card-playing scene, I love that.

I haven't started my periods yet. I don't suppose I will for a couple of years. I'm small for my age and skinny – that's because of my heart. I have to stay skinny so my heart can cope with my growth. Mum says it's a Protective Mechanism.

Summer has breasts and everything. I don't care really. Except that then she sort of began to be bitchy and whispered behind my back – said I had anorexia not a heart disease – and before we moved she had started to see lots of Janine and Rosa. But I expect that was a sort of protective mechanism too – getting ready for when I left.

My heart has to work really hard just to keep me sitting still. I've heard it through a stethoscope – it sounds like an express train going through a tunnel. Scary, really. I'll have another operation, one day, I expect – when they've found a suitable donor. Which means that someone has to die first, someone whose blood type, tissue type, etc matches mine. It's an amazing thought, someone else's heart and lungs being used by me.

Will I have their feelings? Will I have their heartbreak, their heartache, their heartstrings? What are heartstrings and what does warm the cockles of your heart mean? (A Grandpop expression. Maybe because he lived in Shoeburyness, and that's where they get fresh cockles from the mud.) Will I feel heartless? If the donor is – was – older than me, will I be suddenly wiser or more stupid? Like when cannibals eat the brain and heart of an enemy. Do they do it in order to have the benefit of the dead person's experiences? Will I be aware of having part of someone else in me? Maybe it's a sort of rebirth for the donor. Like being born again.

I wonder if the dead person's parents will be happy, or rather, less unhappy, that their child's heart will still be pumping for someone else. I would be.

I think if I died and some of my organs could be used to benefit some very ill person, they should be used. I don't suppose any of my organs are good enough. Apparently, I have an enlarged liver etc. Perhaps they could learn something though – the doctors – from my problem. I would be sort of living on then, wouldn't I, my organs examined by medical students time and time again. Why not? Sounds a good idea to me. If I die.

I was once used as a model patient at the Great Ormond Street Hospital for Children. I had to go with Mum when I was about six and sit on a chair in my vest and knickers, and the paediatrician described my symptoms and asked me and Mum questions, and all the young doctors had a listen to my chest and back and had to guess what I had. I think because what I have is a rare condition they take a special interest in me.

CHAPTER TWO

THIS HOUSE HAS got really ancient Ladybird books with learn-to-read stories for kids where boys do butch activities with their fathers, like camping and building things, and girls get to help the mother in the kitchen or knit a tea cosy. Can you believe it? It must have been terrible in the olden days, having to wear a skirt all the time and remembering to keep your knees together so you don't show your knickers. Mum says they're a piece of Valuable Social History of life since the Second World War.

(Ladybird books, not knickers. Though I expect they are too.)

'Get the door, Gussie, I'm in the bath.'

She's always in the bath. Don't know what she does to herself in there. She always looks just the same as she did before she went in, except that her hair is wetter when she gets out and her face is shiny.

'Hello, Postie.'

'The name's Eugene.'

'Eugene? I thought that was a girl's name.'

'What sort of name 'ave you got then? Gussie? What's that

short for – Angus?'

'No, it isn't, actually. It's short for Augusta.'

'Augusta! Huh!'

'Gussie, what are you doing being rude to the postman? He's come all this way to deliver our letters and you're rude to him. He'll throw our mail over the cliff if we aren't careful.'

'Nah, she's all right, she's all right. We're just getting to know each other.'

Mum is standing there in her dressing-gown with a towel on her head. She has no shame.

'You must keep very fit running up and down this hill every day,' says Mum, eyeing him up and down.

'Training for the London Marathon,' says Eugene and runs back up the steps. He delivered a birthday card from Daddy – *Sorry this is late, Babe, hope you liked the flowers – buy yourself a pretty dress*. A dress? No way! Fifty pounds! Riches beyond my wildest dreams! Mum says she'll take me to Dorothy Perkins in Truro tomorrow.

Today I'm wearing the cool jeans and the sky-blue T-shirt Mum bought me for my birthday.

Summer sent me a card too, from Italy. At least she remembered. Mum says the Postal Service here is Lousy. Summer says she won't be coming to stay before the autumn term starts. And she promised me, the cow. She'd probably hate it anyway. No designer shops, no stars to bump into in the streets of St Ives. She'd hate this house, I know, it's not sophisticated enough for her taste. It's got odd dining chairs and odd crockery and holes in the wooden walls where draughts come through. She'd probably refuse to sleep on the sofa bed too. She can be a bit Princess and the Pea sometimes, Summer.

Still, I'm very pissed off that she's not coming. I cried when I read her card, but I didn't let Mum know. She gets rather emotional at times, and I try to keep her happy. Life's easier that way.

The floor boards are painted black and there's white or cream curtains or blinds on all the windows. None of them match, some are in heavy fabric and some in thin cotton, but it doesn't matter, the sunlight gets through them and wakes me in the morning. The house faces east so we get good sunrises. I do find the climb up the hill to the car hard. We have to cross the railway track to get here, which I think is cool. There's this little train – well, it's full size but only one carriage – that trundles by once an hour or something and goes *toot toot* when it gets near the crossing. It's like being in *The Railway Children*.

Mum is making a herb garden outside the kitchen door. I don't see the point of it if we're moving, but she says she likes to plant things wherever she is. And she likes to use fresh herbs, and she doesn't like the prices they charge in Tesco's. And when you get the pots of coriander or basil home they immediately wilt and you have to throw them away.

'I'm just going for a little walk.'

'Oh, are you sure, darling? Shall I come with you?'

'No, thanks, I vant to be alone.' I say this with a heavy German accent, but Mum doesn't notice.

'Be careful, darling. Must you wear that hat? Where did you find the binoculars?'

'In a cupboard. I don't think Mr Writer would mind me using them.'

'Who?'

'Mr Writer. I think the man who owns this house is a writer.'

'Don't fall over the cliff.'

'Of course not, silly.'

'Take the little backpack.'

'Mum, stop fussing. I'm not a child.'

This is the first walk I've had here on my own. Mum showed me the short circular route and we've done that a few times, including when we watched the non-eclipse.

She's a bit overprotective, my mother. Whenever anyone came to the house in London with a cold or cough, even if it was a plumber or decorator, she wouldn't let them in, in case I caught it. She says I won't catch colds here. Bloody right, I won't, there's no one within a mile to catch anything from.

I clamber through the tangle of branches – hawthorn, I think – and go out the gate at the far end of the garden. Flo and Charlie have followed me but they're scaredy cats and stay there, gazing after me, looking insulted. They really love it here after London. It must be like being in a small cage and suddenly set free into a lovely jungle full of delicious four-legged and two-legged delicacies, just waiting to be caught and eaten. And they can climb trees and things, after only having had brick walls.

There are palm trees in the garden and tree ferns and even banana trees – in England! One of the banana trees has tiny fruit on it. First there was a huge stalk with a red sort of closed flower on it, then, just behind it, a tiny cluster of bananas appeared, like a baby's hand. Little green curled up fingers.

The coast path runs behind the house and goes all the way round Cornwall, apparently. I don't suppose I'll ever do that walk, even if I wanted to. Mum keeps saying we'll walk it one day. I did used to be able to run and stuff when I was about six or seven, when I was little, but my heart won't let me now.

I've forgotten my sunglasses, but I'm wearing my distance glasses. There's a screeching overhead. It's a very fast moving bird. By the time I've got the bins to my eyes it's gone. There's a smell of saltiness or sea or seaweed, or ozone or something. God,

I miss diesel fumes! There's a light breeze blowing, and the sound of sea. Today it's hushing me all the time, *shush, shush, shush*. There's some chittering and a sort of scritch-scratch noise of little birds, but I don't know what they are.

There's pink campions – I know that, and a very bright blue little flower that I don't know the name of but it's the same colour as Eloise's eyes. Mum says it's about as real as her tits. I'll have to look it up in one of Mr Writer's books – the name of the flower. I think it might be squirrel or squirl, or something.

There's also lots of nearly dead clumps of little pink papery flowers everywhere and some dark pink, mauve flowers in small pagoda shapes.

I wonder what he writes – Mr Writer? Is he a thriller writer, or a poet, or maybe he writes travel books? There is a big locked cupboard of his personal belongings that he doesn't want touched by strangers, but he's left out loads of stuff, like these binoculars, for us to use. They're small but heavy and made of brass and leather but the case is on a strap, which makes them easy to carry. I can walk as slowly as I like without being a nuisance and a liability, which I'm sure I must be when Mum really would like to stride out and have a good energetic walk.

The coast path is still muddy from yesterday's rain but all the people have gone. You can see St Ives from the point but it looks a long way away. The tide is right up and it's a clear sunny day, not too warm, just right. The path runs along the top of the cliff and I can look down into the water. There's a high grassy bank between the path and the cliff, so I don't feel dizzy. I wonder if the water's cold? It looks clean and inviting. There's a load of big white seabirds far out, diving straight into the waves like arrows. They fly across the waves then suddenly go head first, wings folded tight, like a folded-up ship going into a bottle, go splash into the sea, and come up a little while later still swallowing a fish. I could see the splashes the birds made before I could see the birds. I'll look them up when I get back. I should have brought a bird book with me. Next time I will.

This part of the coast path is quiet, but St Ives is very busy at this time of the year.

On our holiday in St Ives before Daddy left we had homemade ice cream, which tastes a billion times better than Wall's, and went on the beach every day. We stayed in a self-catering cottage in the old town – all low beams and dinky little windows. We dried our clothes on a washing line in the tiny front garden, which was about one square metre, and Mum thought they would get stolen but they didn't. There were window-boxes with geraniums in and lots of cats wandering around and even walking in our door as if they owned the place. At least, one ginger cat came in once and made itself comfortable on the doormat in the sun.

I didn't go swimming much, but I did love splashing about just where the surf broke on the white beach. If you lie down and put your ear to the beach, you can hear the surf booming through the sand. There were lots of coloured windbreaks and umbrellas and people lit barbecues in the evenings and watched the sun go down. Teenagers and little children all playing cricket, and grannies and parents, all together, and friends. And bigger children looking after the little ones and the babies. And everyone happy. It was so cool. I'd like to live there forever.

Our cats would love to live there too. Much safer for them than London, and lots of other cats to make friends with or yowl at. But now they've had a taste of nature red in tooth and claw out here on the cliffs, I don't suppose they'll be happy settling for less. Daddy says they've got brains the size of a pea, so maybe they forget where they've lived once they've moved house.

CHAPTER THREE

Note: Blaring. It's called blaring – the noise cows make when they've had their calves taken from them. I just found it in this old book called The Care of Farm Animals. *Blaring. And the name of the little blue flower growing on the cliff is squill. I was nearly right.*

I'M HAVING A lie-in today. Mum says I overdid the walking yesterday. I like my bedroom, which is all white-painted wood, and I like the way the sea reflects on the ceiling in little shifting stripes. I could get hypnotised just concentrating on the flickering light.

You can tell where the tide is by the waves on the ceiling. It must be right in up against the cliffs. It's strange how the sound of the sea is loudest when the tide is a long way out. Now there's just a hushing sound, which is really soothing actually. If I sit up I can see right down to the shore, but I feel a bit breathless and woozy today, so I'll probably doze some more.

My bed is very old – metal-framed, with a pretty bed head

and foot end of twisted and knotted cast iron or something, and I have a lovely patchwork bedcover which is all different bits of cotton fabric, spots, stripes and flowers and very girlie, but I don't mind. Mum says it has character. She's right. There are wooden planked walls too. There's a little cracked mirror with a leather frame with a hole pierced in the top so it can hang on a nail. I've never seen a mirror like it before. It must be ancient. There's another large mirror on the wall opposite, an ordinary frameless mirror, but circular, like a porthole, with metal clips on the edges.

There are hundreds of books in this room. When we first came here and the windows had been closed for a long time, the house smelt of old books, like a second hand bookshop or a library. It's a lovely smell, sort of musty and cobwebby. I wonder why old books smell that way. Is it the bookworms?

The books are mostly about nature – birds, wild flowers, lichens, mosses, grasses, trees, mammals, sea shore creatures, butterflies and moths. There are loads of old novels. And travel books, and books all about Cornwall. There's almost a whole wall of poetry books. There's even a *Winnie the Pooh* in Latin, *Winnie Ille Pu*. Maybe I could teach myself Latin from it. I love *Winnie the Pooh*, it's one of my favourite books of all time. I hated *Alice in Wonderland* – mainly because of the illustrations, I think, whereas the *Winnie the Pooh* drawings are somehow just right, comforting and cosy. Also because I found the red and white queens rather creepy and the adventures were scary: Alice suddenly becoming very large or very small.

I remember when I was little and lying in bed in that strange place between sleep and waking, I used to have this weird sensation sometimes of growing larger and larger until I filled the entire room and it was as if I was floating over the bed and seeing myself little and lying there but I was also this huge being looking down.

Daddy's flowers are next to my bed, a tight little fist of vivid colour, sharp and foreign looking, just like the packed bunches of carnations they sell in the street in Spain, except the Spanish ones smell smoky and peppery and sort of wicked, like cigars, and these have no scent at all. Everything else here is bleached to pale pastels. The white walls take on the colour of the sea and sky depending on the weather, but even when it rains the house is bright and you almost have to wear sunglasses inside. At the moment one wall is grey-green and the ceiling is the colour of a gull, a pearly white.

There's a high shelf that runs all round the room in here and another in the sitting room. Plate shelves, Mum says. The wooden brackets that hold them up are shaped and pierced like sunrises or sunsets, like you get on some gates on old houses. He's left lots of old plates here, the owner, plates shaped like fish, in pale green or yellow, flat fish with silly faces and little fins in a different colour. We don't use them to eat off though, in case they are precious.

There are also some paintings on the walls, not prints but real oil paintings and watercolours. Seascapes and landscapes, all Cornish scenes, I should think.

When the wind blows hard, the whole house shakes and trembles and draughts come through the wooden walls and floors, and I keep expecting the fishy plates to leap off the wall. Mum insists I have a window open at night but I have to shove a paperback in the gap to stop it rattling. We only use books we haven't enjoyed, and never the books that belong to the owner.

It's exciting to be here when there's a strong wind blowing. The rooks look like broken umbrellas or black tattered cloaks, thrown away and tumbled by the gusts. The gale shaves the tops off the waves and sends the spray flying back into the sea. And big waves come up over the rocks below, onto the gun emplacement, or whatever it is. It's dangerous to get close to the sea when there's a big swell. Every year, anglers get swept off the rocks and drowned. I can't remember where I read that. Maybe in this book I'm reading by a man called WH Hudson. *The Land's End*, it's called, – *A Naturalist's Impressions in West Cornwall*. He was born in South America and travelled around this part of Cornwall in the very early years of the twentieth century. He reckoned the Cornish were a race apart – 'Celts with less alien blood in their veins than any other branch of their race in Britain.' He also said that the Cornish 'were like the Spanish, passionate.' And that 'Celtic cruelty is rather due to a drop of black blood in the heart – an ancient, latent ferocity which comes out in moments of passion.' Hmm!

Mum used to take me to tropical countries in winter when I was little. We've been to Kenya three times, Thailand once and the Seychelles once.

We also went to the Canary Islands with Daddy one winter. A monkey attacked me. He was an organ grinder's monkey on a long leash and he saw me walking towards him and attacked me, grabbing at my jacket and pulling it off my arm. I screamed and screamed but I wasn't really hurt, just a tiny scratch on my arm, luckily. Mum said they had wondered whether to get me to a doctor so I could have rabies injections, but the skin wasn't broken so they didn't. I think they've stopped people keeping monkeys like that, as part of a street act. I hope so, it's so cruel keeping them tied up.

We went to a circus in the Canaries and the posters showed elephants and lions, and tigers and snakes, but there was only one baby elephant, a dancing dog, and a few mangy lions in a cage that looked like it was going to topple over. The lion-tamer looked terrified and all he could do with them was stop them killing him, which I suppose was enough. It was funny in a very scary way. And there was a woman who nearly fell off a tightrope, she kept wobbling, and then she was fired out of a cannon, except it didn't work and she sort of fell out instead. But I liked watching the audience best. The old men in black flat-topped broad brimmed hats and with wine in pigskins or something, pouring the wine from a height into their mouths; and the women with wonderful fans to keep themselves cool. Daddy bought me castanets and a folding paper fan. I wonder what happened to them. And all the little children wore white – white dresses or shorts and white crocheted socks and white sandals, and they all looked so cute. Mum bought me some Exquisite Garments there, she says. A sailor suit dress with stripes. I don't really remember that. I hate dresses.

'I'm off, Gussie. Now are you sure you'll be all right? What can I get you?'

'For goodness sake, Mum, I'm not ill, just tired, that's all. You know I like mooching. You can buy me some Smarties.'

'Please!'

'Please.'

Mum's going shopping to Truro. I was going with her to spend my birthday money from Daddy but I'll have to do it another day. Even the thought of walking up the cliff to the car makes me feel exhausted.

Rambo and Charlie are on my bed, curled up asleep on my cuddly blanket that I've had forever. It's a blue and pink checked woollen blanket that used to go on my baby buggy, and I love it. It might not be exactly the one I had, but it's a substitute one Mum bought when she realised I wouldn't be parted with the old one, and she washed it a few times so it faded a bit and got to look like my old blanky. It fooled me anyway when I was about four. I used to suck my thumb and rub the blanket on my cheek. I still do suck my thumb sometimes. It's a comfort thingy. Mum says my thumb will never be the same shape as the other one. She's right. My right thumb is flatter and wider than the left one. I don't care. I think it makes me look interesting. I like things that make people look different from other people, like scars. Which is just as well.

I'm going to read some more of this old book, which I like for its strange old-fashioned manner of expression. This writer rambles – that is, walks – through our part of Cornwall and sees everything, including the people, with a foreign eye. It's interesting.

There's a big gull outside on the rail of the decking. He's not making any noise, he's just sitting there and looking in. He has a cruel looking curved beak with a yellow spot on it, and his breast feathers are so very white. He has pink legs and webbed feet and he is a very handsome fellow. In St Ives they have gulls everywhere, nesting on the roofs, and there are notices saying do not feed the gulls, because they start taking food out of people's hands, including the hands of small children, who get frightened. But I think they are very splendid creatures.

This man WH Hudson says there used to be lots of jackdaws in St Ives, sitting on the roofs. He liked watching them peering down the smoky chimneys and talking to each other, as if they were trying to decide what was cooking on the fire below. He made friends with some of them, by feeding them, and the local people thought he was very odd. But he thinks the jackdaw is a very intelligent bird and very amusing to watch. I wonder if those big black birds on our pines are jackdaws? All big black birds look the same to me, and they all go *caw* or *wah*, more or less.

There are all sorts of twitterings going on too from small blue birds, small green birds and small brown birds that look like tabby cats. There's so much to learn about everything. Will there be time?

I don't really think about how much time I've got. It Doesn't Do to Worry about things you Can't Change. She's right, of course. But I do worry that I won't have time to do all the things I want to do. I don't know what I want to do yet, but the possibilities seem vast and unending. I thought I might be a vet but all the girls I know want to be vets, so there'll be lots of competition. Most people seem to have quite boring jobs, like solicitors and bank managers and plumbers and secretaries. I'd rather do some exploring or mountaineering or sail round the world single-handed, except that I get seasick and I don't like heights. But that sort of thing, anyway. Perhaps I'll make a list of all the jobs I might be able to learn how to do.

At least I've been to foreign countries, more than most girls of my age. I did love Kenya so much, but I can't go to very hot countries any more. Last time we went somewhere hot – Thailand – I got pains in my chest and arm. When we got back to London the cardiologist, Mr Samson, said I shouldn't really get too hot or too cold anymore. Which is one reason we came to Cornwall – they have milder winters here than in London.

CHAPTER FOUR

A LONG TIME ago, in the days of ancient Greece, this insect was named Mantis, or the Prophet. The peasant saw her on the sun-scorched grass, standing half-erect in a very imposing and majestic manner, with her broad green gossamer wings trailing like long veils, and her forelegs, like arms, raised to the sky as though in prayer. To the peasant's ignorance the insect seemed like a priestess or a nun, and so she came to be called the Praying Mantis.

There was never a greater mistake! Those pious airs are a fraud; those arms raised in prayer are really the most horrible weapons, which slay whatever passes within reach. The mantis is as fierce as a tigress, cruel as an ogress. She feeds only on living creatures.

Having a flexible neck, she can move her head freely in all directions. She is the only insect that can direct her gaze wherever she will. She almost has a face.

Great is the contrast between this peaceful-looking body and the murderous machinery of the forelegs. The haunch is very long and powerful, while the thigh is even longer. And carries on its lower surface two rows of sharp spikes or teeth. Behind these teeth are three spurs. In short, the thigh is a saw with two blades, between which the leg lies when folded back. This leg itself is also a double-edged saw, provided with a greater number of teeth than the thigh. It ends with a strong hook with a point as sharp as a needle, and a double blade like a sharp pruning knife.

When at rest, the trap is folded back against the chest and looks quite harmless. There you have the insect praying. But if a victim passes by, the appearance of prayer is quickly dropped. The three long divisions of the trap are suddenly unfolded, and the prey is caught with the sharp hook at the end of them, and drawn back between the two saws. Then the vice closes and all is over. Locusts, grasshoppers and even stronger insects are helpless against the four rows of teeth. (Fabre's *Book of Insects*)

I wish I had had this book with me in Kenya. I could have studied the mantis. And now I will never again have the chance. Bother and poodlebums! That's one of Grandpop's expressions that were supposed to be swear words. They were much more inventive and amusing than any real swear words. He never said anything rude – except bugger and damn – Grandma wouldn't have allowed it. She was very religious and proper. Unlike my parents, who say sod and shit and fuck but never the 'c' word. Mum says it Demeans Women.

I do miss them, Grandma and Grandpop Jackson. They lived in Shoeburyness, in Essex – which is a long way from Cornwall but quite close to London. They used to think of the best things to do when I saw them – like play Monopoly or Scrabble, if it was cold and raining, or chess, and Grandpop cheated like mad, and Grandma got cross and we always ended up killing ourselves laughing. And when it was fine we used to go for walks along the seafront and talk to very old friends of theirs who had a little wooden beach hut called Happy Days, and who offered us fish paste sandwiches and cream buns and disgusting tea from a flask. And these people never nagged me about how I was getting on at school or what I wanted to be when I grew up. They didn't whisper about how frail I looked, and never looked at me as if they were sorry for me. They treated me as if I was normal, not some sort of freak. They just wanted to laugh and chat to Grandma and Grandpop, so I could just go and balance on the black wooden breakwaters and find white stones on the pebbly beach to rub together to make a spark. I think they might have been quartz pebbles.

I've found a very powerful magnifying glass in the house, and I'm sure we're meant to use it. It was with the binoculars and it's quite ancient, with a fancy ivory handle and a circular metal frame. But it's rather large and much too good to carry with me when I go out exploring. I'll try it out in the garden first, when I'm feeling better.

Fabre says, 'many a time, when Mantis-hunting, I have been clawed by the insect and forced to ask somebody else to release me.' That's extraordinary, because, when I rescued the mantis from the loo it made no attempt to attack me. It must have known I was helping it.

The cats have shoved off. I was moving too much; they didn't appreciate the earthquakes. It's funny how they often come and lie on my bed when I'm not very well. They seem to know when I need affection and company. I'm lucky with my cats.

I think I might be a scientist when I grow up – an observer of animals and insects, like WH Hudson and David Attenborough. Better even than a vet.

Our gull – I call him our gull because it's the same one who comes each day – is the ghost of my Grandpop. Mum told me Grandpop always said he would come back as a gull. He was a sailor and everyone knows that sailors come back as gulls. She calls the herring gull Pop, which isn't a very beautiful name for such a handsome bird, but I've started to call him Pop too. He is very well mannered, for a herring gull. He doesn't shout and scream for food, he simply waits patiently, for hours sometimes, usually on the roof or the deck rail, until I find him a little treat – sometimes it's only a crust of bread, sometimes a bit of bacon or old cheese that's been sitting in the fridge for ages. As soon as I open the kitchen door he flies down from the roof and looks eagerly at me. He is so beautifully clean and white and his back is a sea blue-grey. I would like my walls painted in his colours, when I have my own room in our own house. He is the only 'character' I see all day, mostly, apart from Eugene, who usually runs down the hill to us, quickly posts the letters through our letter box and runs up the hill again.

Mum says Eugene's Dishy in a Brutish way. I can't see it really, except that I do quite like Bruce Willis, and he is rather brutish, I suppose. I don't know why I like him but I think he has a beautiful soul as well as being tough.

I like Kevin Costner too, but he isn't quite so tough seeming. I loved him in *Waterworld*. I've seen it four times. Everyone else thought it was rubbish but I loved it, all those Heath Robinson sailing boats and machines and the smoking baddies on jet-skis – cool. I liked *Rollerball* too, except for the boring love bits, and no one else did. Maybe I've got rather odd taste in films.

Pop is very amusing sometimes. He stands outside the sliding glass door and taunts the cats by pecking lightly at the glass until they either turn tail and slink away, or face up to him and lash out, spitting at the glass. I'm sure they know they can't get hurt with the glass there, but it seems to me rather brave of our little cats to stand up to a bird that's bigger than them, and with a long sharp beak.

I have decided to keep a notebook of my observations of Pop and other herring gulls.

I have a lovely new book with a shiny green cover, hardback, with blank pages so I can draw things as well as write notes. It was an extra birthday pressie from Mum. It's almost too beautiful to spoil with writing in it. And there's a ribbon so I can go straight to the page I'm working on. And I've bought a new pen, especially for my notes. It's a liquid ink roller and makes my writing look very grown-up.

Mum has started a part-time job with a local estate agent. Just on Saturdays. She reckons that she will be the first to get to know if anything exciting turns up in the way of a suitable house for us to buy, and she's always been nosy about people's houses, so this is the ideal job for her. And I can phone her at work if I need her in a hurry.

She lives in the past, but I suppose all adults are like that.

She has this awful habit of speaking in capital letters, like everything she says is vitally important. I usually ignore her. I do talk to the cats. Only Charlie talks back to me. The others are silent. Good listeners though. I have just remembered something about the real Pop – he called Grandma 'Mate', and until I was quite grown up I thought that was her name. In their house the floor was always called 'the deck' and I learned my port and starboard before I knew left from right.

Today the sea seems bigger than usual. The waves are sort of wintry and… broiling, I think the word is. I don't think I like the sea very much. It's just too… big!

CHAPTER FIVE

Note: There are so many different sorts of gulls and I can't tell the difference between them really, except I know what a herring gull looks like, because of Pop. He's a mature male – larger than the female – you have to see them together to tell that the male is heavier and bigger than his mate. The young ones are brown and speckled. In St Ives they are all over the roofs, making a great racket, all squawking and wheezing and hunching their shoulders like they've got asthma, and the very young ones jump up and down flapping their virginal... or is it vestial... wings? They hang about for weeks being waited on by their parents who regurgitate fish and chips and pasties for them to eat. I wonder if they suffer like humans by eating rubbish? All those E numbers.

Pop hasn't brought a female to our house to nest. He must be a bachelor or a widower, or maybe he's gay. I wonder if they have homosexual gulls?

Last year's young are all flying together and learning stuff from the mature ones. They gather at sunset on our beach and listen to one or two mature gulls and go off together and rise on the thermals. I think they're learning how to fly and gather food and chase hawks. I've seen them go really high.

I'M MUCH BETTER today so I've got a backpack – very lightweight – with a bottle of water, an orange, a banana, a Mars Bar (yum), and a pocket book of bird identification. And of course, I've got Mr Writer's binoculars around my neck. And I'm going for a nature walk. Mum is sunbathing in the garden. And I've got my new notebook and pen.

I've already seen a stonechat, I think it was – it makes a noise like a stone scraping on another stone or a chalk on blackboard. Sort of crich, crich!

Last night I read right through *Jonathan Livingston Seagull* in one go. It's very short. I think it's about religion really, or maybe just about trying to achieve something special in your life – a sort of philosophy. It's about this gull who doesn't want to be part of the flock, he wants to be the best, fastest flier of all time, and he goes off on his own to do just that, and I think he dies and goes to heaven but I'm not really sure, and then he teaches other extraordinary gulls to do what he has done. Anyway, since I read it I've been watching the gulls more carefully, and it's true, there are gulls who only seem to be with many others in a flock, doing whatever everyone else is doing, whether it's scavenging in the harbour or flying out to sea to sit on a load of fish, and then there are the unusual gulls who seem to fly on their own, the individualists. Maybe they are more like people than we think.

It's a very beautiful coast path, this, with pink heather blooming and bright yellowy gold gorse, which smells lovely – like Ambre Solaire or something. There's only the sound of the sea.

It makes all sorts of sounds. Like breathing. It's like a great alive beast, breathing heavily sometimes, and then other times it's panting, or coughing, or even sneezing and snoring loudly. Mostly it just sighs heavily the way I do when I'm really fed up about something. (Fed up – where does that expression come from? Why does it mean miserable?) But the sighing sound is quite relaxing somehow, and so is the whole background constant sound of moving heaving water. Good for the soul, as Mum says. I like the little waves that have white lace on them and that make pretty patterns on the sand. And I love the bluey, greeny turquoise of the shallow water and the way it turns deep blue, navy blue, and dark jade green as it gets deeper. Not like the horrible brown-grey of the Thames at Shoeburyness where Grandma and Grandpop lived.

I wonder how slowly water has to fall before the sound is a torture? How can the sound of a leaky tap or a drip from a broken gutter drive you mad, but the constant gush of a waterfall be soothing?

And sometimes the sea booms like a drum and huge waves bash the cliffs, crashing into them as if the ocean is trying to move them out of the way so it can carry on into the whole land, take over the countryside, and the villages and towns and cities and make everything into sea, which is a pretty terrifying idea, and might well happen even here, what with global warming.

I should think dying by tsunami must be the most awful way to die. Imagine that giant wall of water coming straight at you. Would you run? You would run, of course you would. How would you feel? Does your whole life really flash before you, when you know you are going to die? Who said that, anyway? How does anyone know that that is what happens when you know you're going to die? Like that story you used to hear at school. That dream about falling down stairs – if you don't wake up before you hit the bottom, you die. Well, that's stupid. How can you know you're going to die if you don't wake up? What I mean is – how can someone who wakes up know what will happen if she doesn't wake up? No one ever dies and comes back to tell us what it was like, do they? Oh, it's too confusing and stupid.

And think how the poor cats would feel if there was a tidal wave. They hate water, except Charlie, who always comes into the bathroom with me when I go to the loo and sits on my lap, and gets on the edge of the bath when I'm in it and pats my wet head, and drinks from the bath water, leaning right over, only her back legs hanging on the rim of the bath. I know she'll fall in one day. She'll scratch me when she panics. She loves me so much, she can't bear to be away from me, and knows she's my favourite. Every morning she rushes into the bathroom after breakfast, if I go anywhere near, even if I'm not going in there yet. She's so funny and sweet.

I think I've seen a chaffinch, which has a pink breast, and a pair of stonechats, and I've definitely heard a skylark. They go crazy, flying higher and higher, flapping their little wings like mad, and singing all the time. There are more of them here on the sand dunes than further along on the rocky path that runs along the cliff edge.

I like this bit, because I can sit down on the tussocky grassy sand and read, and have a rest. The path further along, nearer the house, is too narrow to sit down on.

I wish I had a dog with me. A dog would chase birds though, and I'd have to pick up the poo and put it in a plastic bag – yuk! Perhaps a dog isn't such a good idea. If only the cats were brave enough to walk with me. I think Flo might be. Maybe I'll test her out – try little walks at a time. But if she meets a dog, what could she do? She'd be terrified.

Note: The blackbirds here in Cornwall are not as good at singing as the ones in London. Really, I've noticed. They sound sort of wooden and stilted as if they are just beginning to learn to play the piano. I suppose London blackbirds have expensive private education that includes music studies, and are sent, eventually, to the equivalent of the Royal School of Music. And local blackbirds have to learn their music from their parents. So if their parents don't have very good voices, the young won't know how to sing properly. Life's not fair, even for the birds.

Another bird observation: our pigeons, I think they are rock pigeons, but they hang about in our trees, don't know how to fly. They just think they do. They know what they're supposed to do, flap like mad and swoop, but they suddenly fold their wings back and sort of stall, like a little paper plane. They drop, flapping their stubby wings like mad trying to gain height until they find a suitable branch or rock to land on. But it's a very clumsy effort at flying, I must say. Grandpop used to make me paper planes when I was little. I've just remembered that.

CHAPTER SIX

Note: Found a beautiful little nest on the path, it must have fallen out of a tree in the wind or something. It's empty – no eggs or baby birds, thank goodness. (Does that come from 'thank God'?) There is a book on nests and eggs here of course, so I've looked it up. It's small and rounded and neat, and made of tiny twigs and hair and fine strands of orange string, and lined with what looks like long fair dog hair, or human hair, and on the outside there are tiny bits of green lichens like pebble dash on walls, and moss woven in. It smells of damp moss, like a florist's shop. There are one or two tiny feathers inside, so maybe there were babies and they've flown. I think it might be a chaffinch nest. Another book says chaffinches are also called pink spink, twinck, and tink, because of the shrill note of the male bird. And in the autumn it sings 'tol-de-rol, lol, chickwee-ee-do,' the first few notes uttered somewhat slowly, then more rapidly, and a final cadenza at the end.

I WONDER WHAT I would have done if there had been babies in the nest, if they were nestlings with no feathers. Would the parents have come back to feed and care for the chicks if the nest fell out the tree? I don't see how they could really, and a cat could find the babies if it was on the ground. If I found an injured bird, could I ever kill it to put it out of its misery? How would I manage? Do they survive if you try to feed them?

'Mum, what would you do if you found a baby bird that's fallen out of its nest?'

'Put it somewhere safe away from cats and hope the parents come to look after it. And keep the cats indoors.'

'What if it's got no feathers on?'

'There's a bird sanctuary in Mousehole, near Penzance. I'd take it there.'

'Is there? Can we go there sometime to see it?'

'Some time. Anyway, Gussie, don't go Looking for Problems before you've got them. We've got Enough Problems already.'

It's Sunday and Mum always takes me to the local car boot sale on Sundays. It's a great place to find old books – not that we need any more old books – and homemade marmalade, and clothes that people don't want any more (but some are very Decent and Cheap), and plants. Mum has started doing more in the garden, since she's had such success with the herbs, so she's decided to make her mark on the wilderness, as a thank you to Mr Writer.

There are some very sad people here at the car boot – people who look very poor and sort of crooked and with missing teeth. I've never seen so many people with crutches and walking frames and even wheelchairs, and double buggies and dogs, usually very big dogs or Staffordshire bull terriers or Alsatian dogs wearing masks. Muzzles, I mean. Some people bring two or more dogs with them and always stop in the middle of a narrow bit to talk to other people with dogs, so you can't get by easily. And some of the people speak in such a broad accent I can't understand anything they say. It's like a foreign language. And the local men call each other 'my lover', or 'my handsome', which I think is sweet of them. One old man called me 'my flower'. I felt all soft and fluffy and feminine. I liked it. It made me feel sad all over again about Grandpop.

Mum has bought three red geraniums in plastic pots and from the same man I bought another very long bird feeder that can hang from the copper beech tree with the other one, and a large bag of sunflower seeds. The birds get through a whole feeder full each day. The man sold trays of mesembryanthemums – which Mum said she used to think were called messy bums when she was young.

The car-booters who sell plants all seem much friendlier than the other traders. I wonder if working with plants makes you a happier person? Or maybe they are lonely because they work with plants and not people, and that's why they are pleased to talk to people. It must make you patient I should think, growing plants, because you have to wait such a long time to see the results of your work. I wonder if it's like that when you bring up a child. Except that you do sometimes see people being horrid to their children, so maybe it doesn't make you patient at all. Maybe it makes you the opposite of patient. Cross and fed up.

London parents seemed less tolerant of their children than parents who live here. I think people who live here have a better life in many ways than Londoners. They breathe cleaner air for one thing. They don't bump into each other in the street all the time – except in the summer – and they don't have traffic jams so much, except on bank holidays.

I really would like to go into St Ives and sit on the beach and watch the sun go down. We don't see it from where we live.

That was my favourite thing about being in St Ives. We sat

against a high wall on the beach, facing the sea and sun, all of us wearing baseball caps, and Mum and Daddy drinking wine, and I was allowed cola – which I'm never usually allowed because of the E numbers. I get quite silly, apparently. It must be like feeling drunk. And Mum and Daddy were nice to each other and even held hands, and I made friends with some other children who lived there and they let me play beach cricket with them, even though I was only four or something, and they were very kind. One boy showed me how to catch properly, not snatch at the ball. He was so good-looking and tanned and at least ten years old. I wonder if I'll always be attracted to older men because of that?

Grandma used to play cricket in a men's team with Grandpop. She was the only woman in the team. I never saw her play; she was too old by the time I was born. It's so cool, having a gran who played cricket in a men's team. I think she used to run a women's team but it fizzled out.

They both loved to watch cricket on the telly, especially the test matches. I can't get up much enthusiasm, but I do like the white clothes, and it's sort of a peaceful thing to do, watch cricket, and if I'm angry about something it makes me calm down. Perhaps they should use it in anger management – that's what some men have when they've abused their wives. I read it in the *Independent*.

It's just as well I don't want to be a footballer or tennis player or a marathon runner. I might be very unhappy if all I was interested in was playing energetic games, because I know I can't. I am much more interested in reading things and looking at things around me, and learning about animals and birds and insects. So my heart problem isn't really much of a nuisance. Yet.

'Mum, can we go into town and sit on the beach?'

'No, Gussie, I don't feel like it.'

'But Mum, why can't we go? I'm sick to death of being out

here in this lonely place. I need to see people. I'm going bonkers, talking to myself.'

'It's so bloody difficult finding a parking place.'

'Oh Mu–um. We could take a picnic and watch the sun set.'

'Oh, all right, if you really want to go.'

Cool! She's finished planting the geraniums in large clay pots on the deck. They look stunning, so vivid, like fresh spilt blood. Such a foreign colour. They smell like cat's pee.

Note: There's a wild flower that grows on the dry-stone walls in St Ives – Valerian – that comes in dark pink, medium pink and white, and when it's rained they smell absolutely disgusting – like dog shit. And the smell always fools me and I have to look under my shoes.

This beach we're having our picnic on – Porthmeor – is sort of big and white with a green hill at one end with a little house on top. It's called the Island, but it isn't actually an island. It's not so busy at this time of day. I think the holidaymakers mostly go back to their hotels and self-catering cottages to wash and dress to go out for the evening. Only the locals are left on the beach to watch the sun go down, and a few surfers, there's always a few surfers. Mum looks cool in her white baggy linen trousers and black vest and a black linen cap. She always looks good, and I feel proud of her when we're out together.

'Do you remember being here with Daddy? We sat in the exact same place.'

'Do you miss him Terribly, darling?'

Mum's finished the bottle of red wine that she brought with her, so I suppose she's feeling maudling (look that up when I get back to make sure it's the right word).

'Not really, Mum, only sometimes.'

She has started to cry. An ashy tear appears below her sunglasses and runs down the length of her cheek next to her nose. I get up and walk away. Buggering Nora, I should never have asked that question. I wander down to the water and splash about at the edge and look back surreptitiously and see her blowing her nose on her paper napkin. It's red – her nose. Now I feel my throat getting tight and sore feeling. And I think I'm going to cry too. Oh, bugger everything!

But I can't be expected to handle grown-ups' emotions. I am, after all, pubertal. I have troubles enough of my own. I used to think puberty was called pubberty because it meant you were old enough to go to the pub. To be exact, I'm not actually pubertal – but pre-pubertal. No hairy armpits or breasts or anything yet. But I feel my hormones beginning to range, I think.

CHAPTER SEVEN

I'M ON THE coast path next to the house when I see this interesting looking woman.

'Hello!' The woman I speak to has short blonde spiky hair, almost punky, but she is too old to be a punk – twenty, at least. Also she's wearing sensible walking boots and a black sleeveless padded jacket. She's got binoculars around her neck. So have I.

'Hi,' she says.

'Are you a birdwatcher?' I know I shouldn't ask questions of strangers, but she looks OK, smiley. And I haven't seen anyone to talk to for ages. She says she's keeping an eye on a peregrine falcon's nest.

'I know they're protected.' I put my borrowed bins up to my eyes and try to look as if I know what I'm doing.

'Those look antique,' Punky says. 'Here, have a go with these.'

I can't believe how light they are. 'They're cool,' I say and hand them back to her.

'Did you see the nest?'

'No.'

She points at a black bit of cliff with a low shrub growing out of the base of it.

'There's a narrow ledge there, under that leafless bush. Look again with my binoculars.'

At that moment the peregrine flies past us and glides in to her nesting place, and I get to see the landing.

'Wow, that is so cool.'

'There's one chick, did you see it?'

'No, is there?'

We stand side by side and look at the mother bird's back. She settles down on top of the chick, presumably – I can't actually see a chick. After a while my bins get heavy and I leave off looking at the bird.

'Is this where you live?' She nods her head towards our ramshackle shack.

'Yes, sort of, we're renting it.'

'Lucky you! It's got the best view for miles. You must be able to see the dolphins.'

'Dolphins? We haven't been here long, we haven't seen any yet.'

A hang-glider appears over the top of the cliff behind the peregrine's nest. The man is like a huge blue bird, part of the fabric of the hang-glider, spread out, face forwards, with a crash helmet on. Punky puts the bins up to her eyes at once and focuses on him. I think he's seen us. He has. He glides over us, right above us, and I feel like I'm being spied on. She keeps on looking straight back at him. He moves past us fast and makes a slow turn at the point and heads back towards the highest bit of the cliff, up near the farm where in April I heard the cows crying for their calves.

'Do you get many hang-gliders here?'

I tell her they often fly low over the house and garden and Mum hates them – says they are Violating Her Privacy.

The hang-glider has disappeared over the brow of the hill now.

'I better be off,' she says. 'Nice to meet you.'

'What's your name?' I call after her, and then feel stupid and like I'm still a kid. Child, I mean. (Grandma said kids were baby goats.)

'Ginnie,' she smiles at me. 'Police Constable Virginia Witherspoon, actually. I'm in charge of wild-life welfare. You can call me Ginnie if you like. What's your name?'

I tell her Gussie.

'Perhaps, Gussie, you might let me know if you see anyone trying to disturb the peregrine's nest. Just call the St Ives police station and ask for me.'

I watch her as she strides away. Wow, a policewoman in charge of wild animals. That must be really interesting. What a cool job to have! And she could be American Indian with that name – Virginia With a Spoon. She did have a rather strange accent, sort of sing-songy. I wonder how that name came about? Perhaps an ancestor was the first person to make a spoon out of silver. They are very good at making things out of silver. And turquoise.

I realise then that she's asked me to help her, just like that. Keep my eyes open. Just call and ask for her. I feel suddenly taller, which is cool, as I'm very small for my age. Mind you, Mum and Daddy aren't terribly tall, so I haven't much of a chance of being a model.

I remember when I first noticed that Daddy wasn't as tall as other fathers. It was on a path by a river, I don't remember where, just that it was a sunny day with puffy white clouds, I must have been about six, and there were boats and swans. A man he knew stopped to speak, and this man was so much taller than Daddy, and I had always thought Daddy was the biggest, tallest, most powerful person in the world, and suddenly I saw that he was rather short really. Daddy had to strain his neck to look up at the face of the man, like a baby bird does when its mother is feeding it. And I had this awful feeling, which I can't describe really, but it was horrible, as if I had been tricked, somehow, and had just realised it. I know all sorts of short men have been famous and powerful – Napoleon for one, and Tom Cruise, and Humphrey Bogart, and Nelson, I think. He's still my Darling Daddy, anyway. Of course he is. It goes without saying. What a very strange expression that is! *It goes without saying.* Huh! What goes? Where does it go?

'Mum, I saw the peregrine and I know where it nests.' Mum pretends to be impressed but I don't think she's too interested in the local bird-life, really. She's reading some stupid magazine about clothes.

'Someone showed me the nesting place – a policewoman. She's a wild-life warden too. Mum, she asked me to phone her and tell her if anyone disturbs the nest. It's protected.'

Mum is dressed in her dressing gown. She says she had to put her clothes on when the hang-glider flew overhead. She was Not Pleased.

'Mum! You know you shouldn't sunbathe in the middle of the day, anyway. The sun's rays are carcinogenic.'

'Life is Carcinogenic,' says Mum.

CHAPTER EIGHT

Note: At the feeder this morning – a family of greenfinches. They eat very slowly and carefully, standing on the perch, usually two at a time, and chewing away at the sunflower seeds, occasionally looking over their shoulders. One male blackbird drinking from the galvanised bath that's full of water. It was my idea to put a branch across it so the birds can perch on it and lean over to drink. Blue tits, great tits – they are twice the size of blue tits and have beautiful distinctive markings. Dunnocks (which are lovely, like tabby cats) and a robin, feed on the ground. They are 'ground-feeders' – that figures. The blackbird likes apples and plums and pear cores.

I had to go out and bring in Charlie – she was pretending to be a bush under the feeder, not a very green bush, I have to say, before any of the birds came for breakfast. I suppose she thought a little bird was going to drop into her mouth, just like that.

It's been a very exciting day altogether, nature-wise. We were sitting outside having a lunch of egg sandwiches when the peregrine came and perched in the tree in front of us. We had to sit very still so as not to frighten it off. I didn't have my bins, unfortunately, but I could see it anyway. It sat there while Mum's cold wine got warm. But she was very good about it and nearly as excited as I was. It flew away behind the house. Perhaps it was hunting for food for its chick.

HAVEN'T SEEN GINNIE the policewoman at all.

'Mum, do you think I should phone Ginnie and tell her about our sighting of the falcon?'

'Who's Ginnie?'

'The wild-life warden, Ginnie the policewoman.'

'Do you think she'll need to know that?'

'Well, at least she'll know it's still alive.'

'Go on then.'

I phone the local police station and they say she's not there but they'll tell her I called.

I have a new pair of binoculars. I paid for them with the money that Daddy gave me for my birthday. I wrote a thank you letter of course. I hope he won't be cross that I didn't buy a dress. He does like me to look pretty-pretty. He doesn't seem to realise that I'm not a girlie sort of a girl.

Mum says he'll want to take me out with him to dinner and stuff and Show me Off when I'm older.

Why doesn't he want to do that now?

He's gone off somewhere on holiday with The Lovely Eloise. Tuscany, I think. Mum says he's got a String-fellow Complex, whatever that is. I hope it doesn't hurt.

I'm off out with my new bins. They are so light, I can't believe it. They are 7 x 25, whatever that means. The man in the shop did explain but I've forgotten. He was very helpful and kind and says they are the best value Japanese binoculars around and have excellent lenses. They are much smaller than Mr Writer's bins and made of black rubbery stuff, but I mustn't drop them or the lens will shift. I can adjust the focus very easily, not like on the old ones. I still have to remove my specs first though, which is a drag. But I've put them on a string too, so I can remove them quickly if I spot a bird flying by.

I think everything should be on strings. I think I might invent a whole life built on strings. Strings for glasses, and bins – OK, that's been done. And cameras. What about strings for drinks, for notebooks and pens, for diaries, strings for keys, for asthma inhalers, for medicines, for money, for credit cards, for books. You could have a sort of special book-shaped folder on strings, so you change the book that goes into the holder. Strings for lipstick. 'I Can't Survive Without my Lippy.' Yes, I'll invent one for Mum. Maybe I'll be an inventor.

I've got one of the bird identification books with me, natch, and my notebook.

It's a beautiful day, so calm and blue, with those little fluffy clouds you always get over the sea, but there's hardly a person to be seen on our beach. We get a few groups of walkers on the coast path, always carrying those spikes you use on a mountain, or on snow slopes, which I think is a bit over the top, but they are usually old people, so I suppose it's better than walking along with a Zimmer frame. Or crutches.

We also get a few surfers, but apparently, according to Eugene, there's better surf in the winter on this beach. I saw a horse cantering along the beach once. That must be lovely, to feel the wind in your hair as you are racing along next to the sea – except the rider was wearing a helmet.

I always wanted a horse when I was little but we never had enough money, we didn't live near a stables, etc. Anyway, I had an imaginary herd of wild horses, which was probably almost as good as the real thing. I invented it when I went to stay with Grandma and Grandpop once for a whole week on my own. My personal horse was a black stallion called Thunderhead. Grandpop read a newspaper with horse racing on the back page, and I used to go through it to see if there were any interesting names I could add to the list. I had a whole notebook full of horse names. It's funny, I can't remember any of them now; I only remember Thunderhead. He had about a hundred mares in his herd, at least. I do remember Silver Star was his favourite mare. I had a little bike with those things – staplers I called them – so I wouldn't fall over, and I got Gran to fix a skipping rope to the handlebars, like reins, so I could pretend it was Thunderhead.

I made jumps in their garden out of boxes and brooms and mops and things and went round jumping over them as if I was on a horse and I was the horse at the same time. Aren't little kids funny?

Actually, I got into terrible trouble over my imaginary horse. I was going to Sunday School at the time, (I realise now it might have been because Mum and Daddy wanted to go to bed on Sunday afternoons for a siesta or maybe a fiesta, and wanted me out of the way). Anyway, one day the teacher asked us little ones if we had any pets. At the time we had Flaubert, but she was older than me and I certainly didn't think of her as if she was a pet – more like a grumpy aunt. So, before I knew it, I announced that I had a pony called Thunderhead. Well, the teacher believed me and so did the other kids, and I found I had to make up stories each Sunday to keep up the pretence.

It was getting beyond a joke. In the end I was winning rosettes in gymkhanas, for goodness sake, and I suddenly realised that God was watching me and listening to my lies and I would definitely not get to Heaven if I carried on. So I killed off my imaginary horse – at least as far as Sunday School was concerned. I put on a very sad face one Sunday and said he had died of a bad cough. It was amazing how they swallowed it. I must have been a really good liar. It's frightening, really. Perhaps I should be an actress.

Soon after, we went on a Sunday School trip to the London Zoo and some of the mothers came too. I had completely forgotten about the Death of Thunderhead, when the teacher said to Mum – 'So sad about Augusta's pony!' And of course the whole dreadful truth came out. Mum laughed sort of, but I could see she was upset really and very cross with me. When we got home she gave me a really good telling off for 'Lying in Sunday School,' and I cried bitterly. I felt so guilty. But honestly, I just hadn't thought when I first said it; it just came out, and then it was too late. One small lie and you're damned! Eat one small foot and you're a cannibal. Sent to Purgatory or Hell or whatever.

I'm not sure I believe in any of that stuff any more. What an awful sort of a God would send a baby to the everlasting fire just because no one bothered or had the time to christen it before it died! I think Heaven and Hell are here and now, in this one and only life, and if you are good and kind to people and animals it makes you feel good and angelic, and if you are bad and cruel, and hurt people and animals, no one loves you and it makes you hate yourself, and that's a sort of living Hell. I think the idea of God is very nice for little children and the idea of going to Hell if you are naughty keeps them in order, which isn't a bad thing, while they are learning how to behave.

But it's a bit like Father Christmas or the Tooth Fairy – all in the imagination. That doesn't explain why lots of grown-ups believe in God or Buddha or Allah, though.

It's too complicated. There don't seem to be any books on religion at the house, so I don't suppose I'll ever find out, unless I get to learn something at school. But we'll only get to learn stuff that's in the curriculum, I think. I've read that somewhere – Mum's *Independent* probably. That's an interesting newspaper. Intelligent, compared to Grandpop's paper. Smaller print and no tits so it must be good.

(Mum tried to get the local newsagent to move the tabloids to the top shelves with the sex magazines, but he wouldn't. She said they Demeaned Women. And small children would see the naked girls on the front covers and think that women were Pieces of Meat or Men's Toys. I don't really see the connection between meat and toys. Also, I was terribly embarrassed at Mum making a fuss.)

Also, they have poems in the *Independent*, which I think is really cool. Death, war, politics (boring), sport, and poems. I think I might start writing poetry. Well, I did some at my first school, but that was just juvenile stuff. My next lot will be sophisticated and sensitive and mature. The results of vast experience – having divorced parents, grandparents who die. Having a life-threatening disease – that sort of thing.

How does anyone find time to do everything they want to do in their life? Life's too short. I suppose the thing to do is to do it now – get started with whatever – just do it.

Poetry is a way of talking about things that frighten you. I read that in one of Mr Writer's books. I wonder if his books are on the shelves – the ones he writes – Mr Writer?

CHAPTER NINE

WHEN WE FIRST came to Peregrine Cottage there was a gardener who came Saturdays to trim the hedges and strim the paths. Mr Lorn, his name was (great name for a gardener), a man with a lovely smile and a straw hat, and he wore a grey tracksuit with holes in the knees. He was bent over a bit but very agile, clambering up the steps and mending the rustic arches – there are several in the garden and they are made of old bits of branches that keep rotting and falling off. He's supposed to be looking after the garden while the owner's away. I've only seen him twice. I don't know what's happened to him. Maybe he's died.

Since then the garden has become rather overgrown – in fact it's more of a wilderness than a garden, I would say. You can still just about see the paths and steps but stuff has taken over. Brambles grow faster than you would believe – there's a bramble branch with thorns shooting out over a path, where there was none yesterday. It's a real thug. Taking over. There are other weedy plants – they must be weeds because they grow so well – with sticky bits on their prickly leaves, and they grow through real cultivated plants and end up looking just like them, as if they are deliberately camouflaging themselves so they can survive.

Note: I've looked them up – Cleavers, they are called. Which is an excellent name because that is what they do – Cleave to me darling da da da da da da... How does it go?

'Mum, what happened to the gardener?'

'I haven't the faintest idea, Sweetie. Why?'

'Because nature is taking the garden back.'

'Hm, I suppose it Is, rather.' Mum is lying on her tummy on a mattress in the sun.

'Is it all right for it to do that?'

'Don't nag me, I'm Relaxing.'

'But won't the owner be rather cross if he comes back and finds he can't find the house because of the brambles?'

'Gussie, you do exaggerate. It's summer. The Growing Season.'

I've noticed my finger and toenails grow faster in the summer, come to think of it. But I hate my fingernails. They're flat and square, like spade heads. It's something to do with my heart condition – spading or something. My fingers too, at the ends. I suppose I'm not a very beautiful specimen of homo sapiens at all, actually. Skinny and small with rather blue skin, limp mousy hair, and glasses. Still, there's not much I can do about that at the moment, so I'll concentrate on my mind.

Education is the answer. I've missed out on a lot of school but I reckon once a person can read, they can learn anything they want to know. It's just a matter of knowing where to go for the information.

I do like novels, because they tell you about how other people live, what they think and experience, and I think that's very important. It puts your own life into perspective and gives you ideas and makes you think of all the things you could do. Unless it's a crime novel, and they are simply entertaining, I suppose, an escape from boring everyday life.

Daddy likes crime novels.

But I think if I read enough of all sorts of books now, when my brain is growing, I'll be able to learn easily. Children's brains are like sponges, apparently. I think adults aren't terribly good at learning new things – like Mum with the metric system and computers and mobile phones and the video. As soon as we find a house to live in I shall ask Daddy to buy me a computer. A laptop would be cool, and a mobile. Then I can talk to Summer whenever I like.

Dream on, Gussie.

CHAPTER TEN

Note: Pop ate from my hand, practically, this morning. I gave him the leftover cat food. They are so fussy, these cats; only eat certain brands of cat food and turn their noses up at others. So, when they don't eat it I can give it to Pop. He is a living dustbin.

THE ORIGINAL POP – my Grandpop – had the most amazing tattoos all over his arms. Mermaids and galleons and roses and eagles and ribbons and dolphins, all in red and blue and green ink, but faded, and his hands and arms had big veins on like snakes, but not scary. And his clothes were scratchy. He sat in his rocking chair; I used to climb onto his lap and we'd rock together. He wore white shirts with no collars and with the sleeves rolled up. He had these cool, silver, elastic armbands that he wore over his shirt-sleeves, above the elbow. He smelt of tobacco and sometimes I'd find a hand-rolled cigarette tucked behind his ear 'for later.' He taught me how to roll them. You take a thin sheet of Rizla paper, lay a few strands of tobacco on it, bunched up. Then you roll the paper around the tobacco and make a trumpet shape – it was supposed to be a cigarette shape, but I could only get a trumpet shape. Then you licked the edge and stuck it together.

Mum doesn't know he taught me that.

He kept boiled sweets – pear drops, usually, in paper bags in the boiler cupboard. They were always stuck together, and very difficult to pull apart. He thought I didn't know about them but I did. I have a very sweet tooth and can smell out a Smartie at fifty metres.

Mum's nail varnish remover smells just like his pear drops. Whenever I smell it it's as if Grandpop is here in the room, with a bit of Rizla paper stuck to his chin where he cut himself shaving.

He kept his tobacco on the mantelpiece in a tin shaped like a ship's capstan. And there was a clock shaped like a ship's wheel, and three black elephants, and two brass pagodas.

In a high cupboard there were piles of old photographs in a basket with a lid, and I'd go through them with him. I couldn't recognise Grandma, who used to be this rather pretty young woman, slim and smiling, with flimsy stuff dresses. (What a pretty word – flimsy). He was a slender young man in the photographs – which were all black and white, and some of them had faded into a pale brown. He wore a white naval uniform and was very handsome. The brown hat he gave me was his first hat after he left the navy – his civvies hat, he called it. It was a bit big for me of course, but he sewed ribbons on it so I could tie it under my chin. That looked OK when I was a cowboy, cowboys do have strings for tying their hats on and sometimes they wear them on the back of their necks.

After he died, (actually, they died at about the same time) I took off the ribbons and wore it properly, in his memory. Mum thought it was morbid. I still have the pencil case Grandpop sewed for me too. It's made of strong white canvas with a zip. He sewed it all by himself. Sailors are good at making things and looking after themselves. He used to do all the sewing and ironing. He couldn't cook very well, though. Mind you, Grandma wasn't such a hot cook either. Unless you like pigs' trotters – yuk! And rabbit stew. She had a pressure cooker that was always exploding. Well, I thought it was exploding. I realise, now I'm older, that it was probably just the valve that kept blowing off the top and all the steam came out in a rush and a horrid whistle. I was terrified to go in the kitchen.

They kept chickens in the garden, and I was allowed to collect the eggs from the shed where they slept. Grandma raised them herself, buying one-day old chicks and keeping them all warm in a big box with a light bulb in the middle. They used to huddle around it – a mass of yellow feathers, all chirping together. Once, one of the chicks had a broken leg and Grandma put it in a splint with a bandage round it. But a fox got in and ate it. Only the bandage was left. I don't understand how the fox didn't eat any of the other chicks, but it didn't.

'It's survival of the fittest, that's what it is.' That's what Grandma said, anyway.

I pretended that one of the adult chickens was mine – a beautiful pure white cockerel that I called King. I used to carry him around the garden as if he was a kitten. He was so soft and light, and pure white with a red floppy crown – his comb, it's called. He crooned to me, *chook, chook, chook*, very softly, like he was purring. I loved him. He was my only pet.

Grandma was a great gardener. Grew all her own fruit and vegetables – potatoes, peas, runner beans on tepee frames, carrots, strawberries, loganberries, gooseberries. You name it, she grew it. It was my job to gather the glowing potatoes when she dug up the droopy old plant. The earth filled with the pearly treasure.

I used to walk around the garden with King in my arms crooning to me, and show him the ripe soft fruit and the neat rows of beans. The chickens were allowed to run around pecking at anything they wanted, they were only shut up inside their shed at night. I was sent out to pick a bowl of gooseberries, or a bowl of loganberries, or black currants or red currants, and I could eat as many as I wanted.

One day last summer, after Daddy left, we went to Grandma and Grandpop's for Sunday lunch, and it was chicken. At Christmas-time Grandpop used to wring the neck of whichever chicken was ready to eat and hang it upside down, still with the feathers on. I didn't like to go in his shed then. A pool of blood, black on the floor; a horrid smell like rusty metal that got in my throat. But this was summer. So, anyway, this roast chicken was tasty and tender and I had lots of roast potatoes – my favourite vegetable, and peas fresh from the pod. I had uncooked peas, I preferred them to cooked. Grandma wasn't any good at cooked veg – half an hour for cabbage, that sort of thing.

So, I was half way through my chicken wing – my favourite part, if it's got crispy skin, and I suddenly had this dreadful thought.

'Grandma? Which chicken is this?'

Everyone went quiet and all the grown-ups looked at each other.

'Grandma? Grandpop? It isn't... it can't be...'

I pushed my nearly empty plate away and stood up and started hitting Grandma as hard as I could around her arms, and she had her hands up trying to hold me off, and I was screaming, 'I hate you, I hate you!' and I ran off into the garden screaming, 'No, no! Not King!

I had eaten my pet. I couldn't believe they could have done that to me.

It was soon after that that I had to go into hospital for my operation, and that's when Grandpop died, and then Grandma died too, and I never had time to say I was sorry. And now I feel awful that the last thing they probably remembered of me was my hitting Grandma and screaming 'I hate you'.

I don't think I broke their hearts. Or did I?

I think they were sorry, but to them the life of a chicken was neither here nor there.

They didn't apologise to me, if it comes to that – *if it comes to that*? How on earth does a foreign person make sense of these silly phrases and expressions? How on earth? I think they are called clichés.

Grandma's kitchen was very small, a kitchenette, she called it, and when she was cleaning rabbits or chickens I used to keep out of the way. The stench of rabbit innards and chicken innards made me retch. I remember the first time I saw the unformed eggs inside a chicken. Like a bunch of pink grapes, strung together. I think I would be interested now in the insides of animals, if I could wear a face mask, but then I was just too young for the experience.

Her dresser – that's a wooden set of shelves above a chest of drawers and cupboards – was full of different sorts of china – nothing seemed to match, maybe a plate or two, but never more than that. I think she dropped a lot, or chipped them on the taps and then they became chicken plates, for the chicken food. She cooked the chicken-food specially – they seemed to have lots of potato skins and oats or something, cooked in the pressure cooker again. That kitchenette was more like a ship's engine room – the steam, the noise, the activity.

She was always busy, was Grandma. When she wasn't gardening or looking after the chickens she was making things –

sewing, embroidery, knitting, crochet, even smocking. She used to make these tiny dresses with smocking on for babies. I had several, apparently. I don't really remember them. I never saw her with her hands still. She made stuff for her local fetes and the Women's Institute. And she was a great joiner. She was a member of everything going – the Conservative Party, the Labour Party, the Salvation Army – maybe not the Salvation Army, but she made gooseberry and strawberry jams and things for their bazaars – anyone who had dances or parties, she would be there. I don't think Grandpa would have anything to do with her friends. She used to dance with other women, all these fat old women in flowery dresses and white curls, dancing together – weird or what? But she always said the same thing when she came back – 'I thoroughly enjoyed myself.'

Grandpop sat at home and watched telly and did the pools. He never won anything, but you had to be very quiet for ages on a Saturday afternoon when they read out the results on the radio or TV. He did win something once – ten pounds – 'Better than a slap on the belly with a wet fish!' He was always saying that. (He said that when the only rent he got for Whitechapel Road was £2.) And 'East, west, home's best.' I suppose if you have been a sailor and sailed the Seven Seas, you get to love your home very much.

I wish I had known them when they played cricket together.

I wish I had said I was sorry.

CHAPTER ELEVEN

Note: There are loads of gannets out there in the sea this morning, diving into the waves as if they've been shot out of the sky. So there must be a large shoal of fish they are feeding on. Actually, I realise I can sometimes see shoals of fish below the house, directly underneath and shifting across the beach to the Hayle estuary at the other end. The shoal looks like a large blue blot. An amoeba I think it's called. It shifts and changes shape rapidly, moving and growing or shrinking like a cloud of starlings when they are going to roost in the evening.

Pop must have come very early for his breakfast. I put out a plate of old cat food last night in the dark and it was gone first thing. But he's outside now waiting for more, or perhaps he's just looking at us, maybe he's studying us. He is so funny when he eats stale bread. He swallows it whole and it gets stuck halfway across his throat. You can see the shape of it inside his gullet.

IT'S VERY STRANGE that people who write in the sand on our beach always write their message in the same place – just where we can see it clearly from the deck and with the letters so we can see them the right way up. I suppose it's just far enough away from the steps and rocks down to the beach so they feel they've gone for a walk, or maybe they want us to read their messages. They don't usually write anything exciting or interesting, though. Only stuff like *Tracy loves Jason* or *Fuck off*. One small fat boy, wearing a red cap and on his own, wrote Fatty, which was sad, I think. Someone wrote *Happy Birthday* but it wasn't to me.

I had a very plump friend once when I was little. She was called Beverley and she had a little sister called Denise, who was just as chubby, and they both wore their hair in plaits. Beverley was a terrible giggler and I once threw a game of Monopoly over her because she wouldn't play properly and kept giggling. I hope she doesn't grow up remembering me as the bad tempered girl with no sense of humour. If I'm famous before I die and she gets interviewed about me she'll say how horrible I was and everyone will hate me. Thinking about it now, she was probably more of a Noughts and Crosses person than a Monopoly person.

There's a little plane that flies across the beach towards St Ives, sometimes, with a banner flying behind advertising various events and holiday entertainments – like *Come to Flambards* and *Visit Paradise Park*. It's a complete waste of time trailing the ads across our beach – there are never more than a dozen people on it, if that. It's the nearest thing you can get to wilderness, I should think, the view from our house. Just sand and cliffs and sky with the estuary and sand dunes and the lighthouse and bay and of course, the sea.

It's about as far as you can get from Camden Town. Not one crusty in sight, no sound even of traffic, no smell of joss sticks and no rubbish floating around in the air. Paradise, some people would think. If you like that sort of thing.

I'd like to go to Paradise Park. They have lots of different species of birds there including eagles and parrots, and they have a breeding programme for rare birds, like the Cornish chough, which is like a crow with a red beak. I wonder, why did they nearly die out? And if they died out, where did people get the eggs to start off their reintroduction programme? And why is it pronounced chuff, and not chow? The English language is a very strange bird.

The gulls here still call at night. As it gets dark – which is very late at the moment, about ten o'clock – they seem to fly towards St Ives, dozens of them, around the point towards the town, to roost on the roofs with their babies, I suppose. Maybe they call to each other so they don't get lost. *Here I am, stay close to me. Follow me, I know the way home.*

When we first arrived here in the spring, there were more bird sounds at night from the waders and estuary birds. I definitely heard curlews calling in the middle of the night.

A mournful sound. No owls though.

Mum is at work today so I have the house to myself. She looked very smart this morning, in a black linen skirt and a stretchy bright pink top. I thought the neckline was rather low, but she said, 'If you've Got it, Flaunt it.' She enjoys meeting people and seeing houses, but she hasn't seen anything suitable for us yet.

I don't even know if I want to stay here, though Mum says it's a good place to grow up in. I don't even know if I am going to be able to start school here in the autumn. It depends.

Summer asked me once if I was frightened to die. She is. But then she's frightened of lots of things – the dark, kidnappers, viruses, eating meat, the Big Wheel, the IRA, Dobermans, hospitals, maths. That's not counting the usual things like spiders, beetles, moths and bats, and snakes too, I expect, but we didn't get the opportunity to meet up with many snakes in Camden Town.

I don't know if I am or am not frightened to die. I think I might have been quite close once or twice – to dying. I don't remember feeling scared then, just very, very tired. And when I had my operation last year to try and help my heart condition, I didn't feel scared, really, just nervous. I didn't enjoy the pain, obviously. But I did enjoy the attention I got from everyone – Daddy especially, and Mum and the doctors. It was as if suddenly I had become special – a celebrity – because of my heart, and people listened to me, as if what I had to say was suddenly important. Of course, they stopped listening once I was out of danger.

The worst thing about the operation was the nightmare I had under the anaesthetic. I was in a huge ball of pain made up of all the people in the world who had ever lived, were alive, or were going to live in the future. I was all the pain in the world and in all time. I gradually flattened out the pain and spread it out to invented people in invented time – as if I was God and had made people in order to share my pain, so I could cope with my small share. It was a horrid dream, and I kept going back into it every time I fell asleep, for about a month. Weird. But it sort of stopped me thinking about Daddy leaving, and Grandpop and Grandma dying.

I think I'm quite philosophical, really. If it happens, it happens. Nothing I can do, so why worry? Just make the most of now. Enjoy life to the full.

I reckon dying will be like falling asleep and not dreaming. Like it was before I was born. Nothing. At least, I hope that's what it will be like. I don't fancy being in a nightmare all the time. I sometimes dream I'm being chased and I have heavy feet and legs, so I can't run; or I'm driving a car and I don't know how to drive.

I dreamt once I was blind. That must be worse than being dead, I think. I would hate to be blind. Though I suppose I would still be able to hear the sea, and stroke Charlie's soft fur and hear her purr.

And I could listen to great music and perhaps I could become an expert on recognising birdsongs. Miss Kezia Stevens, the world-famous birdsong expert. They could take me to a rainforest and I could tell them which birds were there in the high canopy where no one could see them.

Perhaps I could be a famous detective who always gets her man because she can hear things that seeing detectives can't hear. I remember when I was little I used to walk along with my eyes closed pretending I was blind and seeing how long I could go without falling over something.

When I was staying with Grandma and Grandpop I was allowed to go to the seafront shelter near their bungalow and sit with the blind man who always sat there in the mornings. They knew him, so it was all right to talk to him. I used to tell him all about what was going on around him. I never used the verb to see though, in case it upset him. It was very difficult sometimes, knowing what to say and what not to say. For example, there was this very beautiful dog – a Dalmatian – and I described it to him: a tall dog with short hair, white with black spots. But did he know white? He knew black. Or when you're blind is everything a white mist? Sometimes, when I concentrate, and close my eyes, I can see amoeba-like blotches of colour pass over my eyeball, red usually. Maybe blind people get patterns and things they can sort of see.

Rambo just had a sniff of something disgusting on my shoe. Cats open their mouths as if to say Ugh when they smell something they don't like – I read that and then I noticed it's absolutely true. He's so funny – he started sneezing violently.

I can't see or smell anything on the shoe.

Rambo has eyes like gold marbles – you can see the round ball-ness of them, the pupils thin vertical pillars of unfathomable black. His eyes remind me of lava lamps. He's a very beautiful short-haired tabby with longer fur in his ears and long spurs on his front paws and he stretches out like a lion. He has black paw-pads unlike the other two cats, who're black and white and who have pink paw-pads, except they're rather soiled and grubby. I remember Charlie's kitten paw-pads before she ever went outside and dirtied them – like unripe raspberries.

I do love cats. I'm so glad we have sullen, stealthy, silent, elegant pussy-cats whose only sound is a deep purring, and not stupid dogs who want adoration all the time and go *love me, love me, love me, yap yap woof* with their eyes and tongues, and fall over themselves, and thump their tails on the furniture, and you have to clean up after them when they poo. Cats bury their shit.

Mum always says lavatory, not toilet. But once when we were in Spain with friends of theirs they had a discussion about the word for going to the loo, and she insisted she only used the word lavatory, and then Daddy called out to her later and she shouted back, 'I'm on the bog!' We all fell about laughing. She was furious.

There's a big book here called *Roget's Thesaurus*. I thought it might be about prehistoric animals. But it's better than that. All about words. Cool.

I hear a new bird song – not a song, an anxious shout – *dit dit, da da, dit dit dit* – like an urgent Morse Code message. SOS. Find bins, take off glasses, look in direction of sound of bird.

Poodlebums and buggering Nora – can't see a thing. It's more difficult than it looks, this bird-watching, bird-identification lark (not a deliberate pun). Grandpop used to make the most awful puns. He thought he was being very amusing and we had to laugh each time he did it. Grandma said we shouldn't encourage him. She never did.

I have written a poem about Charlie, called 'A Cat is a Poem'.

A Cat is a Poem

My black and white cat is a poem
Purring, leaning to my arm,
Butting her head on mine,
Her arsehole a pursed mouth,
Her antennae in touch with my head,
Her pink toes stretch in ecstasy,
Her fur smells of leaf mould, bonfires,
Damp sphagnum moss, and green tea.

I don't actually know what green tea smells like but I needed a word to rhyme with leaf and ecstasy. It can't be very good because it was too easy. Mind you, I did have to use the dictionary a lot for the difficult words, like sphagnum and ecstasy and antennae.

I have the feeling that even simple poems are difficult to get right. And am I allowed to use *arsehole* in a poem? There's a book here by a poet who uses *fuck* in a poem, so it must be OK. *They fuck you up, your mum and dad*. His words, not mine.

The more I read, the more I realise how little I know, and the more I want to learn it all, or as much as I have time for. It's quite exciting, really, knowing you are probably going to die before you grow old. It means there is no time to waste.

CHAPTER TWELVE

THE BLUE HANG-GLIDER is back, and it's hanging right over the spot where the peregrine falcons have their nest. I've looked through the binoculars but I can see no sign of the birds at the nest, or in the sky. I can't see the nest from here anyway. I have to go onto the coast path to see it. The man is wearing goggles and a black and orange wetsuit sort of thing. He's looking down. He's trying to hover like a kestrel. These binoculars are brilliant. They make me feel as if I am there with him, hanging over the edge of the cliff. But he's much too close to the peregrine nest. They must be frightened by this huge bird thing like a pterodactyl hovering over them. It would serve him right if he fell and hurt himself. I get the camera and take some pictures of him, showing where he is in relation to the nesting ledge. Ginnie will be interested.

Oh my God! What's he doing? He's gone onto the cliff. I can't see him. Is he after the young bird? No, he's dropped! He's lost control and fallen like a stone, his glider like a broken kite crumpled on a ledge on the cliff. He's half hidden under the billowing blue fabric. He's not moving. There's no one else in sight. I'll have to call for help.

'Hello, an accident – ambulance please, air ambulance. Me? Augusta Stevens, Peregrine Cottage, Peregrine Point, near St Ives. Yes, an accident. A hang-glider. He's fallen and is on a cliff edge. On the cliff below the railway track at Peregrine Point, near St Ives. It's difficult to find. No, there's no road. Just the railway line. The branch line. You can see him from here though, yes, Peregrine Cottage. OK, OK. Yes, I'll be here. OK. Thanks, goodbye.'

The hang-glider wing is torn and flapping in the wind. It's blowing over the cliff edge, but the man's not moving. What can I do to help? Maybe he wasn't trying to harm the peregrine at all, maybe he was just curious. The wing is tearing more and now some of it has ripped off completely and is being whisked away by the wind. Should I do something? What? I can't get to him, even if I walk along the railway track. And I said I'd wait here, anyway. And the trains are running. God, I wonder if he's dead.

It's terrible not being able to do anything. Ten minutes go by very slowly. Still no bird. I am taking photographs of the torn sail as it drifts down the cliff. It has snagged on a bush and is stuck there. There are several men in orange jackets on the railway line. They are hurrying towards where the man fell. And here comes a helicopter. It's huge. It's the Navy rescue helicopter. The noise is tremendous. The house is shaking. The men are signalling. The noise is awful. The helicopter is hovering right next to the cliff, our cliff, just behind our trees. Now there are coastguards, firemen, police, paramedics, ambulance people, all sorts of people running along the railway line. They must have stopped the train. They are climbing down to the hurt man, carrying something. There's two people, I think. They're scrambling down by rope to get to him and now they're trying to get him onto a stretcher.

That's what they were carrying. The helicopter is dropping a line to them. The wind is very gusty and the helicopter has to get in extremely close to the cliff. It looks so dangerous. Here's another helicopter, the small air ambulance. It has gone over the top of the cliff, the hilltop above us, where the farm land is and has settled there. The paramedics are attaching the stretcher to the line. The man is wrapped up like a mummy and strapped onto the stretcher and he's being lifted into the air. One of the paramedics is hoisted up with the injured man. They are safely in the helicopter and it speeds away over the bay towards Truro and the hospital. I'm still taking pictures.

It's like a very noisy action movie. Mum will be so cross she's missed it all.

The doorbell rings and it's Ginnie.

'Have you come to see if the peregrine's OK?' I ask her. I feel guilty that I hadn't thought to phone her and tell her what was happening.

'Yes, I'm going to climb up the cliff and see that the nest is still there. Are you all right? Was it you who phoned for the ambulance?'

'Yes, it was. I've been keeping an eye on the nest, but I haven't seen the birds today at all.'

'If they survive that racket, they'll survive anything,' says Ginnie.

I quickly take a picture of her, before she can complain. I've covered the whole event from start to finish and need her portrait to complete the story. She laughs.

'You better give me the film when you've finished it and I'll get it processed for you.'

'It's finished now.' I rewind the film and take it out of its sprockets and give it to her.

She says, 'I'm going to climb up the cliff to get to the nest.'

'It looks very dangerous,' I say.

'I'm a mountaineer, don't worry.'

'Cool,' I say, and she leaves.

Then a policeman calls and thanks me for telephoning so promptly. He says the man has two broken legs and rib damage, but his spine seems to be undamaged.

'He was lucky. If you hadn't seen the accident happen he could have been there all night, or until someone noticed he was missing. He could have died of exposure or something. Well done, Miss.'

I feel my head swelling as he speaks.

Another man comes to the door. It's a journalist from the local newspaper. The policeman knows him. He asks me tell the story of what happened, and what I saw. I tell him I took pictures and that Ginnie has the film. He even takes a photo of me, standing on the deck with the cliff in the background. I don't even notice the height, much. It's so exciting, all this coming and going. I love it.

Ginnie climbs the steep and rocky cliff and has a good look. She is coming down again, safe, onto the beach.

Now, she has gone and so have all the coastguards, policemen, firemen, paramedics, the journalist, everyone.

Back to silence, apart from the sea and the wind, of course.

When Mum comes home, she is totally amazed at the story I give her. She thinks I'm inventing it.

Then on Friday, when the local paper is printed and Mum has collected it from the shop, we see my photographs on the front page, the 'before and after' photos, the hang-glider soaring and hovering, then the broken wing. There's even a picture of me and some of the story as I told it. Mum goes straight back to the shop and buys several more copies. One for Daddy, one for Summer and two for us.

CHAPTER THIRTEEN

Note: A badger came to visit last night. Mum woke me at about midnight to tell me to come very quietly to the back door. There was a big badger eating the cats' leftover food and some old cheese. He was eating very carefully from the metal dish, nibbling neatly and slowly, not like a dog eats – wolfing the food – but eating politely. We had the light on in the kitchen so we could see the badger just outside the door. When he had finished he turned round and went bustling off, his big bum wobbling like a spaniel's. It was so exciting. I've only ever seen a dead one before, squashed on the road. It was much bigger than I expected, but its head was narrow and small, with lovely black and white stripes. I hope he comes again tonight. It could have been a female, of course. I wonder if they look different. I'll look them up.

Another sunny night. Lots of stars – don't have the faintest idea what stars are up there.

DADDY USED TO drive us to see Grandpop and Grandma on Sundays sometimes. He always liked Grandpop and Grandma. Probably because he was an orphan. He was quite old when his parents died, so he wasn't a child orphan. I think he was about twenty. I wish I could have met them. He used to tell me about them, though. His dad sold cars and smoked cigars and his mother wore corsets with bones in them. He says it was like cuddling a tree. And her hair was tight white curls, but sometimes they were mauve, sometimes pink. She used to iron his dad's shirts and take half an hour over each one. A perfectionist. How boring. Mum doesn't ever iron anything. Life's Too Short. Grandpop ironed his own shirts. Grandma, like Mum, was always too busy to iron things.

We always had fun on those journeys to see them in Essex. Mum used to say that we weren't allowed to use swear words when we were at their house, because they were of a Shockable Generation, so we used to get rid of all our day's worth of swear words on the way there. Mum would say, 'fuck and shit, fuck and shit' about a hundred times, and we would fall about laughing.

I love, (loved) going to the old cockle sheds at Old Leigh. I adore cockles. You have them in a little dish with lots of malt vinegar and pepper and you eat them with your fingers, sitting outside at the long wooden benches, and your hair goes in your eyes and mouth, and that night you can still smell vinegar on your hair. Lots of people go there for shellfish – little brown shrimps that you eat by holding on to their heads and tails and biting the rest, shells and all; langoustines, which are very expensive; jellied eels – Grandma's favourite – I don't fancy the grey yukkiness of them; crabsticks – which are totally artificial; proper crabs in their shells, (they are called 'dressed crab'); big pink prawns; winkles – which you eat with a pin, but I don't like

them much because they taste rather muddy; and cockles –
Grandpop's and my favourites, and Mum's. I think Daddy eats
all of them. Grandma would always tell us about how Mum used
to go onto the mud when she was little and collect cockles for
them to cook and eat, and she didn't even try them herself until
she was about my age, when she discovered how delicious they
were. Sometimes we would go for a Rossi's ice cream in an ice
cream parlour. Grandma said there used to be a prettier parlour
on Pier Hill with powder-blue Lloyd Loom chairs and tables,
which Mum loved, and the huge rose-tinted mirror behind the
counter, which made everybody look very healthy and tanned.

We watched the holidaymakers go by – girls with Kiss-me-
quick hats, 'looking for trouble,' Grandma said, 'and usually
finding it'. There was a fortune-teller on Pier Hill and I always
wanted to have my fortune told, but Mum wouldn't let me. We
Make our Own Fortunes. I think I was allowed to go in an
amusement arcade once – on a birthday. But it was so noisy I
didn't like it. I did like Peter Pan's, but I couldn't go on many of
the rides because I was too little. They measure you and if you
aren't tall enough you can't go on, in case you fall out and kill
yourself.

Once, Mum took me out on the mud to gather cockles, like
she used to do at my age. I love the smell of the oil refinery. We
took a plastic bucket and Mum told me how she had a silver
bucket – that's what she thought it was, but of course it was
galvanised metal. She showed me how to find the cockles. You
have to look for little volcanoes with a blue-grey ring around
them. The hole is where the cockle breathes. You dig with your
hand into the purple mud until you touch the hard shell and just
pick it up. It's so easy. They are bivalves and don't bite or anything,
or trap your fingers like giant clams. They are quite beautiful,

cockles, with ridges and mauve stripes. Apparently they jump about and travel a lot when they are young, before settling down in middle age, like people. We gathered half a bucket full in about an hour and took them back to Grandma. She cleaned them in fresh water, then boiled them for a few minute, until they opened. We had them still warm, with vinegar and pepper on, but they didn't taste as good as the ones you get at Old Leigh. Maybe because we ate them inside the house, instead of outside in the fresh air.

We have mussels here, which are great when Mum cooks them. We collect them from the bottom of our cliff. There are loads of them, in colonies, all stuck together like Grandpop's boiled sweets. You have to yank them off and tear out the beard – a sort of stringy bit. It makes my fingers sore but it's worth it. Summer hates all shellfish. She's allergic.

I remember sometimes Grandma wore a neck brace like a high stiff collar. She suffered from her neck and back. And her knees, and her hips, and her hands. She reckoned whisky was the best painkiller, and she and Grandpop had a 'tot' or two of whisky every evening before supper. I hope it helped.

I suffer from poor eyesight. I sometimes see quite ordinary things in an extraordinary way. It makes boring events that much more interesting. Like once I thought I had seen a tiny blue-green fish on a hotel path in Spain. I pointed it out to a maid who was carrying a load of clean sheets. She was totally astonished that I had thought it was a fish. It was an olive leaf. I felt really stupid.

That was before I started to wear glasses. Now I can see everything clearly, more or less.

Pop came as usual this morning, for his breakfast. He made a perfect landing on the rail, balancing with his huge white wings out. I saw him land out of the corner of my eyes. He looked like an angel. Perhaps he's my guardian angel. Not like Clarence, the angel in *It's a Wonderful Life* – 'No man is a failure who has friends.' Like Jonathan Livingston Seagull's guardian angel gull, who was all for being a loner, and not joining the crowd.

This *Roget's Thesaurus* book is very useful. I looked up guardian angel and found: familiar spirit, familiar, genius, good genius, daemon, demon, numen, totem, guardian, guardian spirit, guardian angel, angel, good angel, ministering angel, fairy godmother, guide, control, attendant godling or spirit, invisible helper, special providence, tutelary or tutelary god or genius or spirit, household gods, plus some foreign words – and then ancestral spirits.

Ancestral spirits. Like Grandpop. Maybe Mum's right about Pop the gull.

Why bother sending kids to school when there are books like this? The government could just make sure every child can read, then give every family a lot of good novels and reference books. I don't suppose people can learn maths from books, though. I'm hopeless at maths. Maybe I'll get some extra tuition at my next school, as I've missed rather a lot.

I don't understand why some of the words in the *Thesaurus* are in heavy type and some not.

This is so sad, this bit in the badger book:

Badgers live together in pairs, and are very kind to each other. Two Frenchmen during a walk killed one, which they drew towards the next village. Presently they heard the cry of an animal in distress, and saw another badger approaching. They threw stones at it. But still the creature came up, and began licking the dead one. The men now left it alone, and drew the dead one along as before, when the living badger lay down on it, taking it gently by the ear; and in this sorry way it was drawn into the village, and, I am sorry to say, was killed. (A few badgers are still to be found in this country, but it is not a common animal anywhere. The Chinese consider it a great treat, but in this country no one would eat its flesh.)

CHAPTER FOURTEEN

*Note: A kafuffle on the cliff edge below the cottage this morning.
Two blackbirds and several smaller birds all making a terrible
fuss. I thought there was a pigeon sitting on the tree next to them,
but when I looked through the binoculars I could see it was the
peregrine sitting there right next to the angry little birds, staring
them out. There must be nests down there. He is a dark grey on
the back with a very light chest and black markings on his face.
Wonderful sighting! He flew off without attacking any birds or
getting away with their young. He has sharp wings. I am so happy
the hang-gliding accident and the noise of the helicopter hasn't
frightened them off. They are so brave.*

KAFUFFLE IS A GOOD word. It sounds as if it might come from
India or somewhere foreign. Like bamboozle.

I phoned Ginnie and told her about the peregrine. She reckons
the one I saw might be the young one, trying its hand at hunting
on its own, and she's promised to come out when she can.

The tide is out and there is a large shallow pool at the foot of the cliffs with tiny ripples that look like Grandma's skin. Mum says her skin is getting old. Well, she is over fifty, so what does she expect? She had me when she was forty-one, which is too old to start being a mother, I think. And she will lie in the sun, which is very bad for the skin.

I am an only child, and so was she. I sometimes wish I came from a large family, and had brothers and sisters to do things with but on the other hand I do enjoy my own company and peace and quiet. What am I saying? I don't want just my own company and Mum's. I'm bloody bored with my own company. I want to be with people, lots of people – I'm a townie for Christ's sake, not a bloody countryside freak.

Mum just ignores me most of the time – which is cool. I don't want to be fussed over and organised. One of my favourite things is mooching. Just doing nothing much, daydreaming, thinking silly thoughts that sometimes take me to strange places, letting my imagination go wild, and reading, of course.

One of my favourite times is when I just wake up in the morning – that half sleep half awake state, where you aren't sure whether your dream is reality or not, and even when you realise it's only a dream, you try to hang on to it, finish the story, actually they are usually more like films. I hate it when I wake suddenly and the dream disappears from my memory. Like the very end of *Jennie*, when the little boy who has been a cat all through the book wakes and immediately forgets his friend Jennie, who saved his life and taught him how to be a cat.

That bit always makes me cry.

I would have to give it a different ending if I was the writer.

Mum read *Jennie* to me when I was little and I have read it to myself since. It's quite a difficult read with many long words and sentences but it's a wonderful story, one of my favourites.

Dreams are like films, I think, that come out of nowhere, like switching on a television film. They are inhabited by strangers, sometimes. Where do they come from? Maybe they are really there on another level of the universe, a bit like ghosts, who meet us on crossroads of time and space and, just as suddenly, disappear. Maybe that's what happens to us when we die. We simply get onto another dimension, a parallel universe. Some people who are alive in the present are good at seeing beings from another world or time. And some people never see them at all, or even imagine them.

Mum doesn't dream, ever. She says she's still catching up on all the sleep she missed when I was a baby. I never stopped crying, apparently.

Pop has had breakfast, had a small through-the-glass argument with Flo and Rambo, and has flown off. He'll be back at teatime. I've filled the bird feeders and there are the usual little birds feeding – blue tits, great tits, greenfinches.

I put out bits of old bread and cheese and pasta last night for the badger, but didn't get to see him. The food went, though, so we think he had it.

There was a notice in the local paper for homes wanted for hedgehogs – they've got some at Newquay Zoo. I would love a hedgehog in the garden, but Mum reckons we have too many steps here for a hedgehog to negotiate. This garden is all steps and terraces, like a mountainside farm, except the little dry stonewalls are collapsing and the terraces are becoming slopes. Mum is out there every day now, battling with the brambles, but there's not much she can do really. Everything grows so fast. She's just about Keeping the Jungle from the Door. She looks so furious when she's pulling up the weeds. She says she pretends she's pulling out The Lovely Eloise's hair.

It reminds me of when we were in Kenya and the undergrowth was always cleared around the house, to keep snakes away. I saw an enormous monitor lizard once, on the path between the house and the beach. I was only little and I thought it was a dragon. Mum missed it that time and didn't believe me. But when we were there again another winter we saw one together. It was about five or six feet long – a big one, very close to the house.

I loved the vervet monkeys best. They used to leap from the sausage tree into the scrub, babies clinging to their tummies, making the most awful racket. And I loved the weaverbirds' nests: carefully woven little balls at the ends of palm tree fronds, like green Christmas tree decorations. When the nests became old and torn and yellow, they would rebuild them.

Zakariah – who cleaned and cooked for us – made the best curries, and used to climb the coconut palms and gather nuts for me. He was probably about Mum's age, fiftyish, but he had white hair and seemed very old to me. He lived in a village several miles away from our rented beach house, and had to walk back there in the evening in the dark. It got dark at seven o'clock. He was frightened of losing his trousers to robbers, he said, so Mum said he must go home earlier, while it was still light. One time we had an ayah to look after me, for when Mum wanted to go out on her own. I don't remember her name – and she and Zakariah had a big argument and he beat her, apparently. We weren't there when it happened. The police came and took him away and Mum had to pay lots of money to get him out of jail. The girl kept telling us, 'He bit me. He bit me.'

Zakariah told Mum that the girl was his niece and she was lazy and flirting with another young man who worked close by, so he beat her. Mum looked after me on her own after that.

Mum took me snorkelling every day. I couldn't swim very

well but the mask and flippers helped. Luckily, we didn't know what we now know – that some of the fish, the lionfish and moray eels, were dangerous. We had no fear, so it was like floating in underwater heaven surrounded by fish of every possible colour and shape and pattern. Little orange and white striped clownfish that live inside the poisonous tentacles of sea anemones, protected by the anemone from bigger fish. Yellow and bright blue fish, striped, spotted, zigzag patterned. Imagine all the colours and patterns and shapes of fish that could possibly exist – well, they actually do. They had lovely names too – Picasso fish, surgeon fish, angler fish – that one had what looked like a fishing line and hook hanging from its face.

We were like fish too, just hanging there in the warm clear water. If you trod on a coral head by mistake, a little fish would peck you on the leg to make you get off their territory.

Mum and I were the only foreigners on that bit of coast, apart from a Polish woman who looked after the cottages. We didn't see much of her, because she suffered from malaria and had fevers.

Being there was like time standing still, a paradise on earth. The sun shone every day. We ate bananas, fish, and curries. Fishermen came to the door with parrotfish and lobsters. Dhows with white sails passed on the horizon. There was a reef a mile out and sometimes we walked out to it at low tide to look at the starfish and sea cucumbers, and gather shells. We only picked up the empty shells of course, but we saw loads of live shellfish. There were huge clams tucked in among the coral. When the tide came in, all the little white crabs – they were almost see-through – made a rush for the little waves, and then changed their minds and ran back to the beach. They live in holes in the sand and if you chased them they would sometimes go into another crab's hole and be chased out again. I used to watch them for hours. We found lots of tiny red coral pieces on the beach. They have holes in and we made them into necklaces and bracelets. They were a bit scratchy but very pretty.

Sometimes when we had to go into town to shop, we went into Barclay's Bank to get cool. It was the only place apart from the cinema that had air conditioning. I saw my first ever film in Mombasa – it was *Dr Doolittle*. The grown-ups kept making noise and the children had to keep shushing them so they could concentrate on the film. It was like a huge party going on with people drinking beer and laughing and talking. I thought all cinemas would be like that and was quite surprised and disappointed when I went to a cinema in England.

The only thing I didn't like was going past Mombasa meat market. Yuk – the smell of warm meat. I always held my nose as we drove by.

There was an elderly man staying at one of the other cottages for the whole winter. He walked around in his pyjama bottoms because of the heat. He said he was 'happy with this view and sixpence'. He and Mum used to sit together in the evenings and drink gin and tonic and laugh.

I would love to go back to Africa.

Eugene rang the bell this morning and when I went to the door he had a letter for me. It's from the hang-glider man. He's still in hospital. He says he's very grateful to me for calling for help. Someone must have told him.

CHAPTER FIFTEEN

Note: I have just rescued a bumblebee. It was trapped inside the downstairs room, buzzing about sounding very worried. I managed to get it onto an aquilegia head and put it outside onto a potted pelagonium. It must have thought it had died and gone to Heaven.

WHEN I WAS born I had to have an operation straight away almost, and I nearly died. The Australian surgeon said to Mum and Daddy, 'Your baby nearly went to Heaven.'

Mum said my babyhood was a Total Nightmare.

Luckily I don't remember anything about it. I know I had a dummy and Grandma kept trying to take it away from me. But I don't really remember, it's just that Mum told me that later.

My right-hand thumb is the one I still sometimes suck – only when I'm really, really tired – but I'm actually left-handed. Which is strange. Maybe I write with my left hand because my other hand was always stuck to my mouth. My handwriting is crap.

Mum thinks children should have all the comfort they can

get, whether it's a dummy or a thumb to suck, or a cuddly blanket, whatever. She said she wasn't allowed to breastfeed me because I was too weak to suck at first. I was fed through a tube that went up my nose and down my throat. Luckily, I don't remember that either. She tried to breastfeed me, but I just couldn't suck enough milk to keep me alive. I think she probably feels guilty about it.

Mothers feel guilty about everything, even when they aren't, she says, and if you're a mother You Can't Win.

I think the first thing that I remember about being alive was Grandpop throwing me in the air and catching me. Flying. I was flying and safe. Scared and happy at the same time.

Mum says I need more men in my life. She does, she means.

She used to smoke but gave it up when she was pregnant with me. She's recently started again, even though Grandpop died of cancer. Daddy's never smoked. I wish Mum wouldn't. She says it's her Only Vice these days, and she doesn't do it in the house because she doesn't want to expose me to passive smoking. Actually, I think she drinks too much, too. And she keeps crying. I've seen her in the garden, pretending to dig or something, but her face is all puckered up.

I never did that thing some children do when their parents split up – hope they'll get back together. It never occurred to me. I just thought that was what fathers did – pissed off when they'd had enough, or when things got tough, or when they met someone younger. Most of my friends have stepfathers, or their mums live with a partner who is not the father of their children. We're not so very different. Except Mum hasn't got a partner.

When we live in St Ives she will be able to go out more. I could make friends too, maybe. And when I go to school there I'll definitely make friends. Anyway, I just live for the day. Make the most of every moment in case it's the last.

Note: We are making shell curtains to hang over open doors to stop butterflies and flies and bees coming in.

CHAPTER SIXTEEN

Note: We saw a little baby badger last night. (Perhaps if I open the kitchen door and keep the light on, it will still come, won't be frightened and I can take a photo of it.) Its mother or father came first, about ten o'clock – it was nearly dark – ate the bits of bread, and went. I put out the cats' leftovers in case he/she came back looking for something more substantial. Almost immediately, this baby arrived. It was so sweet – no stripes yet, just the salt and pepper bristles. I hope it comes back tonight. I'll put out some of the cat food that the cats won't eat. They'll only eat the food in sachets these days. God, they're fussy. I suppose they get enough protein from free-range mouse, anyway.

I HAVE BEEN examining Rambo's eyes very closely, using Mr Writer's magnifier. (I'd forgotten about it. I must take it out in the garden.) They are like prehistoric amber – the pale yellow sort with tiny black fish embedded. So there's all this liquid amber, sliding, and the elliptical black iris swimming and changing shape. When he comes in from the dark his eyes are totally black and bottomless.

He sees ghosts, unfortunately. It upsets him. When I pick him up he looks over my shoulder at the corner of the room and is worried by his visions. Mind you, he's worried by everything. Poor Rambo is a nervous wreck. He's fine if you're sitting down or prone on the sofa. But if you walk towards him when he's eating, or if you stand up, he'll run away as if you're going to hurt him. And no one in our family has ever hurt him. He's neurotic. I wonder if he sees people ghosts, or cat ghosts? Maybe he sees Grandpop and Grandma. I really think that when we die we end up in another universe, running alongside this one, and some people cross over sometimes and see each other over space or time, like when you're in a car on a motorway and you see the cars coming towards you on the other side of the barrier.

A dog swam from the rocks below the house today. He had a woman with him who threw something into the sea for him to fetch. He was a good swimmer.

I don't fancy swimming from the rocks – even though the water is calm and clear. I know it's cold. I'm not good at cold.

Even on a lovely evening like it is now, it's cold here after the sun goes behind the cliff. If we were on the beach that faces west, we could be watching the sun going down. There would be children playing and people lighting barbecues, and gulls creeping close to take anything worth eating from plastic bags. Families having fun.

Oh! There's a dolphin! I just saw a dolphin. And another. Three of them. Heading towards St Ives, going past the headland. Big dolphins. And a little one. A whole crowd of dolphins. I can see without the bins, but I've found them and now I see there are at least six of them I think.

'Mum! Dolphins!'

We stand like idiots, watching the dolphins, mesmerised by

them, crying, almost. How wonderful that such huge creatures live in our sea. They survive all the pollution and fishing nets and jet-skis and motorboat propellers and there they are, leaping up and playing and fishing off our beach.

They go off around the headland towards St Ives, and I suggest to Mum that we follow them, so we do. She takes the heavy binoculars and I take my lightweight ones. I go as fast as I can along the garden path, out the gate and along the coast path. She runs ahead. I'm out of breath as I reach her, standing on the cliff edge looking down at the dolphins who have moved across the next beach now, Carbis Bay, headed towards Porthminster and St Ives. I wonder if anyone on the beach can see them. They don't appear to be looking in their direction. We have a great view because we are so high. There are six, I think, and they have white bellies, which you can see when they come right out of the water.

We've seen dolphins! It's like a visitation – like seeing the badgers. I feel honoured to have witnessed the wild animals. We are so lucky. I didn't take any photographs. Things always look so separated from the photographer through the lens, Daddy says. Anyway, I didn't even think about it.

We watch until they're out of sight – in fact they dive and don't resurface as they get closer to St Ives. We walk back slowly, bird-watching as we go – cormorants and herring gulls and a pair of stonechats. Stonechats love to get on a high point – a rock or the highest twig of a bush – and sing. There are butterflies, very tiny, grey blue, and a lovely smell of summer, the yellow gorse – which is more like coconut oil than Ambre Solaire. It is very lovely here – so wild and unspoilt, considering it is so close to such a busy holiday town.

'I'm glad we came here,' I tell Mum.

'Good, darling, I'm glad you're glad.'

I feel happy. Happiness is an odd feeling. Like being opened up inside. As if I have been surgically opened to my heart, which is singing. I hope, if, and when, I get someone's heart, that that person's heart has felt such happiness. I suppose it's what they call joy. A pure, clean, lovely sensation, as if I am in love with the world. Which I suppose I am, at this very moment in time. Make the most of every moment. Well, we are, I am.

Peregrine Cottage feels suddenly like home, whatever home is. It's a strange business, feeling at home somewhere. I never did really feel at home at our last house, where we moved after Daddy and Mum split up. He stayed on in Camden Town while we moved to Chalk Farm, so I could carry on at the same hospital and school. The Chalk Farm house was OK. I just never felt it was my real home. Naturally, I wanted to be in the house where I had grown up, with Daddy. And I never did go back to school, anyway.

I always felt at home in Grandpop's house, with Grandma's cooking smells and the sound of chickens in the garden. I suppose that's where I felt most safe, even though it wasn't my real home. The sound of the kettle whistling. My white cockerel. My den in the old coal shed. I had an old mat, a blanket, a blunt kitchen knife, my cowboy hat and gun, and my herd of wild horses, and Thunderhead, of course.

Grandma paid me for collecting caterpillars from her cabbages. Drowned caterpillars stink of rotten cabbages. I have never eaten cabbage since.

I keep having dreams about trying to get home – an unspecified place, but I'm lost in a strange city, unable to catch a train, without money or passport or a map. Sometimes I can't speak the language or read the street signs. The bus never comes, I miss the train, I'm never able to get home. Why do I keep having this dream? No dream books here, unfortunately. Maybe I'll be a psychologist when I grow up. I'd love to be psychoanalysed. It must be wonderful to talk about yourself all the time and have someone listen to what you say. Of course, you'd have to pay someone to do that.

We don't get many visitors, as we haven't made any friends here yet. But we do get Jehovah's Witnesses. Always the same two, a young man and a slightly younger woman – in their early twenties, I think. Very serious, smartly dressed, she always wears a longish dark skirt. They knock at the door and Mum says, 'I can't spare the time to talk to you now. You'll have to make an appointment to see me.'

She sounds angry.

'Why don't you want to talk to them, Mum?' I ask after they leave.

'They don't believe in blood transfusions, Gussie. If you had been born the child of a Jehovah's Witness, you wouldn't be alive.'

I wonder why they believe that. I think we should invite them in and ask them, but Mum is adamant. She doesn't want to get into an argument.

She always takes one of their leaflets, though. It's called the *Lighthouse* or something. She uses them as cat-food mats when we run out of *Independent*s. Last time they came, we were just on our way out and we walked up with them from the house. There were four more of them standing by the railway line, all in black, like a funeral party, looking over the beach, standing on the very edge.

Mum told them, 'It's Not Safe – people throw their garden rubbish over the edge and it looks more solid than it is.'

Afterwards, when we were in the car, we were hysterical, laughing at the possible headlines in the newspaper if they had all gone over the cliff: 'A Wailing of Witnesses'; 'Jumping Jehovahs'; 'Wipe-out of Witnesses'.

All in the worst possible taste, but we did laugh. Mum can't dislike them that much – she probably saved their lives by warning them about the cliff edge.

CHAPTER SEVENTEEN

FACT. THERE ARE two sorts of worlds.

   1. The World of the Well

   2. The World of the Sick.

You can pass from the World of the Well to the World of the Sick quite haphazardly, depending on luck, mostly, but if you happen to have started life in the World of the Sick, it's difficult to pass over into the World of the Well.

Sometimes a cure is found.

Sometimes a miracle is performed, like a magician's trick.

The heart lifts and blood flows the way it is supposed to.

Last year, after Daddy left and before Grandpop and Grandma died, the doctors opened me up to make some necessary repairs, discovered they couldn't do what they wanted to and stitched me up again. But even though they could do nothing, air – oxygen, flooded the heart and my chest cavity, and found its way into the chambers and tunnels, and moved through all the narrow, dark passages, and the grey-blue fog that had been the colour of my flesh bloomed into a flushed, sun-kissed pink. I looked healthy and normal. My breathing was easier, even though I was stitched from front to back and scarred as if a shark had held me in its mouth and tried to bite me in half.

I felt great for a while.

CHAPTER EIGHTEEN

I TRY NOT to think about it, but I suppose I'll have to sometime. Grandpop dying, then Grandma. I missed it all really. I was either in hospital having my operation, or I was at home, recovering. I didn't get to see him in hospital, and I didn't go to his funeral. And when Grandma died only a few days later, I missed her funeral too. Mum had to deal with it all on her own. The first I knew of Grandpop even being ill was when he was in Southend Hospital having an operation. I was in my London hospital and Mum had to travel between the two to visit us.

When she told me he had died, it was like the worst thing that has ever happened to me. I couldn't believe it. And then poor Grandma, dying of a broken heart a few days later. Daddy looked after me while Mum arranged everything about the funerals. I wanted to go but I couldn't. It was weird, not having Mum there. Daddy isn't terribly good at illness and stuff. But he did read to me, which was lovely. I only wanted children's books for some reason. He read me all of *The House at Pooh Corner* and I couldn't stop crying.

How many days does a woodlouse live? We get lots here, they come in the house, and you find them climbing the walls in the bathroom, keeping to the groove between the tiles. When I try to rescue them to put them out, they don't curl up. The ones in Shoeburyness always curl into tight balls when you touch them.

Herring gulls can live for forty years. I read that here.

Pop comes every day, and every day I feed him. He is brilliant at catching food in mid-flight. He'd make a great cricket fielder. I have started to think of him as if he really is my Grandpop, like Mum says he is. I expect he was a good fielder – Grandpop. Grandma certainly was. Grandpop said she was a brave fielder and not frightened of the hard ball. She made some good catches and wasn't afraid to hurl herself at a fast ball to stop boundaries being scored.

I read somewhere, or perhaps I heard it on the radio, that the world is made up geographically, of all the bones and ashes of all the animals and people who have ever lived. Not many people know that. Cool.

I was sitting on the rocks below the house yesterday evening and I suddenly realised there is only one me – only one Augusta Stevens, and no one else can see inside my head, my mind, or my heart, not really. They can saw through my rib cage and poke about in the flesh and blood of me and stitch me up again, but they won't have found the Essence of Gussie. Only I know me, which is a very lonely thought.

I am Me.

I look at my blue hands, the clubbed fingernails, my skinny legs, my narrow straight feet, (my only good point). I touch my light brown hair and my eyelids and my clammy skin, and I'm suddenly aware of what it's like to be – just to be. Scary. I wonder if everyone else has the same realisation about themselves and the fragility of life. I suppose they all do. It's that, Who am I, what am I doing here and why? moment.

I found this, fallen down behind Mr Writer's desk. It's a poem:

Make use of the things around you.
The light rain
Outside the window, for one.
This cigarette between my fingers,
These feet on the couch.
The faint sound of rock-and-roll,
The red Ferrari in my head.
The woman bumping
Drunkenly around in the kitchen…
Put it all in,
Make use.

I didn't know you could put a Ferrari or a cigarette in a poem. So what would I write, if I wrote a similar poem?

Make use of this tabby cat
Lying across the table,
His regular purr and his curled claws
That don't hurt me when I touch them.
The greenfinch chirruping in the pine,
The white curving wave creeping to the shore,
The coast path zigzagging through the hazels,
The heavy scent of the creamy palm flowers
Leaning against the window.
Cricket on TV – the voice of David Gower.
The curtain of tiny shells to keep out bees and butterflies.
The Mars Bar waiting for me in the fridge.

I could go on and on.

I don't have a godfather or godmother because I wasn't christened. Summer has loads and gets expensive presents on her birthday from them. Not that I need expensive presents – it would just be someone to talk to about stuff. My heart, Daddy leaving us, Grandma and Grandpop dying.

I know old people have to die, to make room for the young, I suppose, or there would be terrible blockages and overcrowding in the world, but I need my old people. I miss them.

Mum is taking me to a poetry reading. I don't know who is reading whose poetry, but I think it's a sort of local poetry magazine thingy. We're eating out afterwards.

I'm bored. I never tell Mum that. She blows her top. Loses her cool. One thing she Can't Stand is anyone saying they're bored.

Hardly anyone ever goes past the gate, or climbs down to the beach. There are no human sounds, only nature. A horse came galloping over the sand towards us. It's a strange noise – like nothing else – the hooves pounding the sand, sort of echoing and much louder than they should be. You can hear the hooves before you become aware of the movement of the animal, when the shape is still just like a small mirage, or a hovering shimmering person appearing in the distance in a desert.

I miss the small back gardens of London; our back garden on a summer evening – the overheard arguments, a violin playing, a piano, blackbirds, the robin that used to sing in the dark, the sound of traffic, the scent of honeysuckle and jasmine on our trellis on the yellow brick wall. Sparrows. Sitting on the fire escape with Charlie on my lap, listening to people chatting in the neighbouring gardens. Laughing. The orange sky at night, planes, heat haze humming over the tarmac. People with no gardens sitting on window ledges on a sunny day, or even on a sloping roof. I miss London – barbecues, curries, bonfires, bus fumes, babies crying, chatty taxi drivers, black people. There's hardly any here. The amazing buzz of millions of people living cheek to cheek. Like ants. Giggling with my friends. I miss giggling.

I was woken one hot night in London by a crowd of men – drunk or stoned, I suppose – talking loudly in one of the back gardens, I couldn't see where. One of them had a particularly cruel voice, though I couldn't hear what he said. It just sounded horrible, frightening. Scary. They talked until after four. I couldn't close the window because it was so warm and stuffy. I should have shouted at them to shut up. Was everyone else sleeping through it?

Then a squadron of geese flew overhead, yapping to each other, and took away the anger I had been feeling all night. It's odd how seeing wild creatures can do that to you. To me, anyway.

Last night I dreamed that there was a shallow pool left by the sea at the foot of the cliff. There were several large fish floundering in the too warm too shallow water. Robot toy soldiers attacked the fish. But the fish were scorpion fish and they fought back with their poisonous spines.

Dreams are weird. Where do they come from? Why do I see places I've never been to, and meet people I don't know?

Grandpop sometimes appears in my dreams, but not close enough for me to see him properly or to talk to him. He's always just disappearing around a corner, or he's in the next carriage of a tube train and I can just see him through the bleary window and he doesn't know I'm there.

Perhaps we sleep *so that we might meet at night our dead*.

How do you say goodbye to someone you love? When Daddy left, he didn't really say goodbye – more of a 'See you later, Gussie Babe.'

I suppose it wasn't really goodbye, anyway. I do see him still.

It wasn't goodbye forever. Not like Grandpop and Grandma.

If I had known they were both going to die so soon, I wouldn't have hit my Grandma and told her I hated her. I shouted, 'I hate you!' That's the last thing I said to her, more or less, as far as I can remember. I cannot for the life of me remember what they said to me.

I suppose the only way to live is, whenever you say goodbye to someone, you must be loving, just in case it's the last time. Though I can't stand it when mothers say 'love you' to their kids even if they're just going to Tesco's. Makes me cringe. But I expect they've already thought about what happens if it's the last time and so they've decided to say 'love you', just in case.

The poetry reading was crap. I didn't really understand much of what was read, all rather obscure with Latiny bits, nothing to do with real life as I know it. Boring. But then something really strange happened. There was this old man, a complete stranger, who came up to me and Mum during the interval and said something to me in Italian. *Cosi* something, something *bella*. Mum asked him to translate, and he said it meant *something lovely is going to happen to you*. I felt very odd, tearful, I suppose, and I said thank you to him. He had a very wrinkly face with smile-lines fanning from the corners of his eyes and white strings holding his lips together at the edges.

We left then before the second half of the poetry performance and went for a pizza in a restaurant overlooking the harbour, with all the holidaying people walking by, and boys on skateboards, and lots of life. I really enjoyed it.

Then we came home. Mum dropped me off at the top of the hill because there was nowhere to park and left me standing in the dark while she drove back to park. I stood there listening to the night when suddenly I heard a scampering noise. I thought the three terriers from the house at the top of the hill had been let out. I'm nervous of them, because they bark at me. But these weren't barking. They came very close before we saw each other. It was a badger and three young ones. The mother saw me and veered away with the little ones following, their claws scratching the tarmac. They disappeared into a thick hedge of a field where there are horses.

Four of them, so close. Mum missed the whole experience. She was very cross. 'Buggering Nora' is what she actually said, after Grandpop.

I expect that's what the elderly Italian man meant. He must have known the badgers were going to appear.

Grandpop used to say, 'Youth is wasted on young people.'

I'm not going to waste mine.

Charlie is sitting on my lap, what there is of it. She loves sitting on me. Usually she sits on my feet in bed, but sometimes on my chest, which is not a very good idea. Her ears are the softest silk, and her long stiff whiskers, some black and some white, are like seal whiskers, with little black spots on her cheeks where they start, like the black spots on the cheeks of old black men, or anyway, the actor that always plays a goodie high-up cop in American movies – I forget his name. Like black freckles. She has little folds on her ears at the back, and her ears are pinkish brown and hairy. And she stretches her paws and each of her four fingers is separated and she never scratches, ever, even when she is scared. And I love her black coal eye make-up. Very Egyptian. I forgot to mention her most extraordinary feature – jade green eyes.

Flo has squirted in the back porch. She must have been frightened or something to make her do such a thing. Cats spray when they are trying to mark their territory. I know a tomcat has been coming in at night. If I forget to cover over the biscuits cats come in for all-night parties. One night, Flo was being chased round and round by this huge ginger cat. They moved so fast they were just a blur. They both flew out of the cat flap eventually. The other two cats were hiding – typical.

I was really worried that Flo would be killed by the big ugly tom if he caught her, but she came back in after about an hour, no damage done. Then the other two appeared and they all walked on tiptoe around the house frightening themselves, thinking each of the others was the ginger tom. I had to groom them all before they would settle down. Flo only lets me brush and comb her head and back. Charlie wants to be groomed all the time. I think she thinks I'm her mother and brushing is like a mother cat licking her young.

It's impossible to tell where the sea ends and where the sky begins today. It's the same grey misty haze all over. The crows are grey blurs flying by. A man disappears on the beach, and then only his legs reappear. We can see Godrevy Lighthouse from here. It's rather friendly – the light going on and off all night; comforting somehow. I imagine I'm a sailor lost at sea and I suddenly catch sight of the beam of the lighthouse. And I'm no longer lost. I can work out my bearings. I can get home.

I've found one of the magazines that the Jehovah's witnesses left. It's called *The Watchtower*, not *The Lighthouse*, but I was close.

Having the sea outside the window and almost surrounding us is like having a guest in the house who won't go home, and won't go and entertain himself. You are aware of the breathing sound it makes, and then you take it for granted and don't hear it at all. Then it gets angry, or seems to – I know it doesn't really – and you hear it crashing about and making lots of noise – the sea and the wind, together – a partnership. Does the sea do what the wind dictates, or is the sea the king of the elements? The sky changes every second. Now it's totally grey yet still bright enough for me to need sunglasses. Now it's blue and pink and green and orange, with thick heavy rounded clouds that are dark grey at the base. And the shadows of the clouds race across the beach. And when a seagull flies overhead, its golden ghost sweeps across the sand.

Perhaps I should take up painting. No point really when so many artists have already done it so well. What can I do that only I, Augusta Stevens, can do? I'm no good at anything. My best subject is English, I suppose. Because I've read quite a few books already. And I quite like acting. And cooking. And animals, but that's not a subject.

Blurt. That's a wonderful word. That's exactly how it sounds when you say something quickly that you didn't know you were going to say but it just comes out – blurt. You blurt it out. Like projectile vomiting. I used to do that, apparently, when I was three weeks old. I had something called pyloric stenosis – which is a blockage that stops food getting into your stomach and causes you to throw up in a stupendous fashion. I had to have to have an operation. That's all I needed, what with my heart failure. I couldn't have a general anaesthetic so they had to tie me down. Mum said the surgeon, who was Australian, said to them, 'Your baby nearly went to heaven.' My heart had stopped during the operation and they had to start it again. Luckily, I remember nothing at all about any of it. Seeing as my heart is so badly designed, it does quite well, considering.

CHAPTER NINETEEN

EUGENE HAS JUST been. He told me he had read all about the hang-glider and said he's seen the picture of me, and he also delivered a letter from the newspaper editor with a cheque for ten pounds. It's for my photographs of the hang-gliding accident. Cool! Perhaps I shall be a photographer, like Daddy, only I'll work really hard at it. I better start right away. Where's the camera? I shall do landscapes first – I don't need to focus for those, just point the camera, turn the distance bit to infinity, and click.

So, I'm standing on the little grassy flat bit just off the coast path and sort of below the garden, with my camera on one shoulder and my binoculars around my neck. I have just taken a few shots of the waves coming right in and over the tops of the rocks. It's very exciting, and I think I have got one or two good pictures. I'm using black and white film – Daddy always said everything looks better in black and white, and I agree.

A boy comes down the steps and he's wearing binoculars too, and just at that moment I stupidly let the camera fall off my shoulder. It sort of bounces and falls down over the edge onto a rocky ledge just below me. I am totally humiliated. Buggering Nora!

I can't reach it, and this boy, who I think is just going to walk straight past me, says, 'Can I help?' And he leans down and plucks my camera from certain death. Death by damp and salt. I'm so grateful I can only stutter thanks, and take it from him.

He's got a really nice smile. Wide and curly mouthed.

'Is it broken?'

I take a shot. The shutter works OK.

'It's indestructible' I say proudly.

He starts to walk away but suddenly sees something and looks through his bins. It's our peregrine, coming right near us. I put my bins to my eyes (after first removing my glasses) and watch too.

I tell him we see it all the time, and as he looks really intelligent and friendly, I tell him where it has a nest. He asks if I'm a birder, and I say no, but I'm willing to learn. That obviously impresses him because he sits on the grass next to me and we watch together.

His name is Brett and he's from Australia originally, and his parents are teachers. They recently moved here and live up on the main road. He's got fair floppy hair and he's sort of relaxed looking and really nice. I show him where we live. Then he says he'd better get going.

Just as he's leaving he asks if I want to go birding with him sometime. I want to say yes, but I don't want him to know about my heart and stuff, and he'll notice if I walk slowly. I don't know what to say. In the end I say, maybe – and afterwards feel really really stupid. But he didn't notice my blushes, I don't think. I hid my face under my cowboy hat. Oh my God, I must look really nerdy. Glasses, funny hat, binoculars, camera, a complete eccentric.

He says G'day – Yes, Australians really do say that!

CHAPTER TWENTY

Note: Two more wonderful words – lolloping and hugger-mugger. Lolloping is a badger's action when it runs away. Herring gulls live hugger-mugger on the roofs. Close together. It sounds like a swear word to me. Like something Grandpop would have said instead of bugger.

The gardener, Mr Lorn, has reappeared. He gave Mum a nasty shock. She was sunbathing 'in the nuddie' – as Grandma used to say – when he suddenly came through the bottom gate into the garden. She only just had time to cover up her rude bits before he was next to her. He has been laid up with a bad back, apparently. He pottered about, and was quite pleased that Mum had done some weeding and stuff. He's rather old for a gardener and seems rather shy. I tried to have a conversation with him but he must be a bit deaf, I think. It is nice to have someone else around. I followed him for a while, asking him about the names of plants, but he doesn't seem to know any more than I do. Grown-ups are remarkably ignorant about the world around them, I find. Mum is, anyway. And Mr Lorn. He has the most wonderful hands – they are gnarled and horny and look as if he is part rhino.

I've just noticed this thing about my hands – not the clubbed fingers, something else.

The lines on the palms. If I place my hands next to each other, little finger to little finger, the lines on the palms match, almost echo each other, except that on my left hand the life line – I think it's the life line – stops half way down, or rather, it is broken at that point and then starts again but in a fractured state, like broken bones, or pick-up sticks thrown down higgledy piggledy.

Higgledly-piggledy my fat hen, she laid eggs for gentlemen. Where did that come from? Probably Grandma.

I think I'll write a story about this palm-reader who notices that everyone's life lines end at the same time or point, except for one or two people, perhaps, maybe even her own life line ends then, and she assumes the end of the world is nigh, so she gets to know the other would-be survivors so they can be together when it happens. It could be a great sci-fi movie. I could make a fortune and leave it to Mum. What could I call it? *Life Line.*

She could buy herself some great clothes and maybe a facelift, except there's no point in a facelift because you have to take off your clothes at some point and then your husband/boyfriend would see your soft and wrinkly belly. I suppose you could wear something flattering that covered all the wrinkly and saggy bits, but bloody hell, what an effort. Perhaps it would be a good idea to marry a blind man. Just keep rubbing in the baby oil and he would think you were young forever. Hope for the best. Whatever. God, the complications of being a woman!

We are putting out badger food regularly now. Peanuts, fish and chips, old bread, anything but salad stuff. They don't eat their greens. They love leftover cat food.

I cannot believe how quiet this lovely beach is in the height of the summer. I suppose it's because you can't get to it by car. You have to walk a long way over dunes through a golf links or along the coast path and down over rocks. It makes it like our own private secret beach, almost.

One of the palms in the garden has leaned over so far it's almost – it is – touching the window and when the window is open the scent is overpowering. Lovely. Exotic. Like East Africa.

I think those days… months… spent in Kenya were the best ever in my entire life. I was very well there. I could breathe. Run, even. Swim – well, snorkel – and it was great. So much wilderness and excitement. Paradise.

Perhaps we all choose our own heaven and hell. That has to be my heaven.

When you see news on the telly of earthquakes and floods and drought and starvation you realise just how privileged you are to be free, living in a boringly calm country where there's no violent politics, no shortage of food or water. You can go out and just do your own thing. There aren't even any malarial mosquitoes here, or poisonous snakes, (except for adders), or poisonous spiders. Or bombs dropping on us. Or lions, or any really fierce animals waiting in the bushes. Perhaps if we had a guaranteed five months of sunshine, England would be a prototype for heaven.

God – or whoever – made it when he was practising. He thought, 'Let's put a green hill here and there, a few white sand beaches, sand dunes, oak trees for shade, bluebells and primroses, foxgloves and buttercups and daisies, but let's have rain and thunder and lightning and dark moors for drama, and birds singing, and a few nonviolent animals. And then let's throw in a few human beings to make things more complicated.'

And the night sky. A bit of terror to make you feel that there's something more out there than you understand, something beyond. A whole universe. And then more.

There certainly isn't time even in an ordinary healthy human's lifetime to learn enough of this world and this life to be satisfied. If I get another chance, I do hope I come back as a healthy intelligent person, who loves knowledge and has the ability to learn quickly about nature and science and literature and astronomy and geology and – everything. That sounds so mushy.

Why are we here, anyway, and why do we want to learn stuff? What good is it if we die just as we are beginning to understand a little of what's going on around us? What is the point?

Here, I mean here at Peregrine Cottage, there is never real silence. Always there's the *hush shush* of waves, and if the wind is blowing, its sound overwhelms even the waves.

I am frightened of the wind. You can't see it or smell it, but it's there, all around you, moving your bit of world, tearing it apart, shifting the roof, pulling up trees, making the sea angry so it gets bigger and bigger and washes you away. The cold east wind I hate. The destructive north wind I hate. The totally devastating south wind – which we hardly ever get – I hate most of all. There were a few horrible storms when we first came here and I was very scared, but I must be sensible about this. I have more chance of dying of a heart attack or stroke than being swept away by the wind, or being in a landslide, or being struck by lightning, or being washed in a tide of mud into the sea, over the cliff, onto the rocks.

Mum isn't working today and we sit outside together and she is peaceful and happy because the heat of the sun is seeping into her skin and bones and relaxing her. Mr Lorn won't be back until next week, so she doesn't have to worry about being caught again without her clothes. I sit close by in the shade, reading an ancient book by Ernest Neal, called *The Badger*, with an illustration of a badger on the cover by Paxton Chadwick – there's another weird name! Where do they get them? The author talks of having to walks for miles in the Cotswolds to find badgers. We have them come to us, literally on our doorstep.

This bit of folklore is a bit worrying though:

Should a badger cross the path
Which thou hast taken, then
Good luck is thine, so it be said
Beyond the luck of men.

But if it cross in front of thee,
Beyond here thou shalt tread,
And if by chance doth turn the mould,
Thou art numbered with the dead.

Does that mean that when the badgers crossed in front of me, it was an omen of my death? But the old man at the poetry reading made it sound like a blessing. *Something wonderful is going to happen to you*, he said.

I take Mum a cup of peppermint tea and she has stripped off, but no one can see from the path, so she's safe. She's rather uninhibited, my Mum. Her body is still good even though she's fifty-two, but she Hates the ageing process. Her eyes don't work properly, and her knees are Giving Up on her, and her Skin Sags. Her bent leg – the skin at the knee bit is stretched and taut, but the skin sort of slips down and gathers at the lowest part of her leg near her thigh. The skin is puckered like beach sand when the tide has left it and little waves are echoed in it. I rather like it. But Mum says, 'Gravity is a Bummer.'

I think having young flesh gives you a false sense of immortality. I don't have that, of course – a false sense of my own immortality. Facing facts, I have probably got another ten or twelve years, maybe a few more if I get a transplant. It seems like a long time to me. Twice the age I am now. Ancient. Actually, the only thing that really bothers me is not being able to breathe very well. Anyway, I suppose I do believe in my own immortality, in a way. I know that I won't be aware of being dead, so I'll only know about being alive. No one remembers before they were born, do they.

This badger book, which was published in 1958, says that there are loads of badgers in Cornwall, and they have sets that go for maybe a mile underground, and that the badgers often make use of deserted mine shafts. Tin was mined in Cornwall in the nineteenth century.

The male badger is called a boar and the female a sow, but they don't have piglets – the babies are called cubs.

There is an account of someone witnessing the funeral of a badger.

A sow had lost her mate. She came to the set entrance and let out a weird unearthly cry; then she departed for a rabbit warren not far distant. There she excavated a large hole in preparation for the body of her mate. She worked at this over a long period, the time being broken up at intervals by journeyings between warren and set. After some hours a second badger appeared, a male. The sow stood still with head lowered and back ruffling agitatedly, and the male slowly approached with head also lowered. Then the female, moving her head quickly up and down, uttered a whistling sound, as though the wind had been expelled through the nostrils; at the same time she moved forward with two tiny jerky steps. When she stopped the male went through a similar motion, his nose to the ground like the sow's. This was repeated. The ritual over, they both retired down the set. After some time they reappeared, the male dragging the dead badger by a hind leg and the sow somehow helping from behind. They reached the warren, interred the body, and covered it with earth. Then the male departed and the sow returned to her set and disappeared.

We look out always onto a watercolour. Each time it's a different painting of the same scene. Now it's a robin's-egg-blue sea with two small scratches – red boats – to the left of the left trunk of the main tree. Now they've met – the boats – merged. And below them, a blue tit on the tip of a hazel branch looks bigger than they do. Every moment the scene changes itself in an effort to produce the perfect painting, yet each moment is, in its own way, perfect and unrepeatable.

There is absolutely no wind, not even the hint of a breeze on the water's surface. It's as if time is standing still.

If only.

You can almost hear the snails sliding up the trunks of the palms to shelter for the night under the dead spears. Tiny goldcrests with their neon orange caps are feeding upside-down on the main tree trunk of the Monterey. I wonder what insects they are eating?

I walk around the garden with the magnifier and look at the lichens on the trees. It's like snorkelling. Lichens have fruits and flowers and look like miniature coral heads. Brilliant.

I find our large toad – a fine yellow warty toad, cool to the touch. He's always to be found in the same place, under a porcelain sink on bricks. It's cool and damp there and he likes it. But if it rains he goes out hunting. There's a tiny pond, very overgrown with weed and water lilies and full of old leaves.

'We must Clean It Out,' Mum says, but I like it just the way it is, all covered over and mysterious. The toad's eyes are tiny golden oranges. If I kiss him, perhaps he'll turn into a prince, or is it only frogs that do that?

Grandpop and Grandma took turn to read me stories, not only when I went to bed but daytime stories too. I loved sitting on Grandpop's lap on his dull green rocking chair, just rocking away gently with his scratchy chin on my face, his cranky old voice in my ear. I can't remember what he read me, really, just the smell of his tobaccoey clothes and the yellow nicotine-stained fingers. Come to think of it, he had clubbed fingers like mine. I never thought of that before. I wonder if he had heart problems too? He died of lung cancer though, I think. All that smoking, I suppose.

Their little bungalow was packed with furniture. A solid and immoveable dining table and heavy armchairs, and rugs over carpets, and a funny old leather cloth on the table before the tablecloth went on. Layer upon layer of stuff. I used to climb onto a stool and then up onto the top of the door to search in the cupboard for treasures – jam-jars of buttons, photos, old clothes for me to dress up in. I was good at climbing when I was six or seven.

'Mum, what's happened to Grandma and Grandpop's stuff?'

'It's in store with our things, Gussie, in London. We'll send for it one day, when I've found a house.'

I went shopping with Mum to a sort of pet supermarket in

Truro to buy cat food and litter. It's only Rambo that uses a litter tray as a loo. We call it Rambo's dunny. (That's Australian for lavatory, loo, bog, whatever. We never say toilet. I don't know why. Most of the girls at school said toilet or loo. Mum corrects me immediately if she hears me say toilet.) It sits outside near the back door. He's scared to go too far into the garden in case a tree frightens him or a blue tit attacks him.

He's such a wuss. All the cats follow me around the garden when I go for a walk. The females fight each other and Rambo follows very slowly, as he has to stop every two steps to look round and make sure the bogey man isn't going to get him.

In the store there was a huge section of aquariums with fresh water fish – not marine tropicals, unfortunately, which are much more colourful and interesting.

There was a bird section too. In one cage, a cherry finch kept trying to escape, flying to the top of the cage, banging its beak or head on the wire mesh and falling back. It was terrible. I told the girl at the checkout desk but she didn't seem to care. Probably working in a pet store makes you callous about animals' suffering. They become merchandise, not living creatures. I keep thinking about it, can't get it out of my head, the poor little bird desperate for freedom.

Also, I can't help thinking about Grandma dying of a broken heart. She and Grandpop had known each other since she was fourteen. All her life. He was her only love. And I was her only grandchild and I told her I hated her.

I have been miserable all day.

CHAPTER TWENTY-ONE

Note: I have decided it isn't like a zoo here – more like a circus! Something exciting happens every day. This morning a racing pigeon with red bands around its ankles walked in the dining room door and made itself at home. The three cats slept on, totally unaware of a bird in their territory – meals on wheels, whatever. Mum was also totally amazed to see it under the table. She put it outside on the deck but it showed no signs of wanting to fly away. She gave it sunflower seeds and peanuts but they were too chunky for it to manage. Eventually she got me out of bed to lend a hand. I suggested putting it in a cat basket with a bowl of water and a saucer of crushed seeds, and then put a towel over the basket so the bird would go to sleep. I remember that's what Grandpop did with their parrot when it made too much noise. Birds go quiet when it's dark – like the gulls did at the eclipse.

Then, after breakfast – porridge and honey – another weird thing happened. I saw what I thought was a seal, quite a long way out. But it was swimming along with its head out of the water, and seals don't do that. So I got the bins and saw that it was a dog swimming – much too far out for a dog – then an actual seal appeared just in front of it, popped his head out, and I saw that the dog was following the seal. The dog's tail was wagging in the water like a rudder. The seal dived and the dog swam in circles looking for it, then it emerged and the dog followed it again. It looked like the seal was leading the dog to a watery grave. I was very worried. There was no sign of an owner. Mum suggested we phone someone – get the lifeboat or something to rescue the dog. I thought of Ginnie and Mum said, 'Yes, a good idea, though the dog isn't exactly wild-life, but never mind.'

So I phoned the police station and spoke to Ginnie. She laughed and said that the inshore lifeboat had been out the day before and rescued the same dog but that it had jumped straight back into the water. It's a Water Spaniel and has a thing about seals.

'Its owner has given up worrying about it,' Ginnie said, 'so you mustn't worry.'

OK. Cool. A dog that thinks it's a seal.

She asked me if I had been watching the peregrine and I said yes and I hadn't seen any hang-gliders or anyone disturbing it. She said she would pop out here sometime and see how the young one was getting on. Cool. I like Ginnie.

The dog eventually gave up on the seal and swam ashore. His man appeared out of the dunes and put him on a lead. The dog looked very pleased with himself – kept shaking himself and wagging his tail.

Life is fascinating here at Peregrine Point. A slow-worm suddenly appeared in the bathroom next to the lavatory. Did it get there under its own steam or did a cat bring it in? It had an old tail-tip amputation scar. I picked it up and put it out. It was much smaller than the last slow-worm victim. It didn't squirm and fight to be set free. It just sat quietly between my fingers. I wonder if it hurts them to be held. Like when you touch a butterfly wing and take off the protective dust. I do hope not.

There was the usual decapitated mouse head on the carpet in the sitting room. I am becoming totally unsqueamish, and pick it up and chuck it out into the garden. Mum can't cope with blood and stuff.

Buggering poodle bums! Should have noted where the head went so I could see if the elusive burying beetles did their thing.

But the most amazing thing that happened was – in the night, a badger stole one of Mum's shoes! For the second time! She had left her very best favourite thick-soled white leather and suede thong sandals, which she bought in a surf shop in St Ives, on the kitchen doorstep – they were muddy. This morning, there was only one sandal. We searched the house, then the entire garden, followed the badger trail as best we could, but found nothing.

Our badger is a shoe fetishist. What does it do with the shoes? The first one was a Hush Puppy backless suede clog – black, soon after we arrived. Mum thought she must have mislaid it somehow. It too was left outside the kitchen door because it was muddy and wet, and she forgot to retrieve it.

Does Brock invite his mates round to look at his designer shoe collection – shoe sculptures, installations, whatever? Does he like the smell or the taste of leather? Are the shoes child substitutes and has he/she lost his/her babies? Does he cuddle up to Mum's two odd shoes? Has he given them names – Hush and Shush, Blackie and Snowy, Black Beauty and White Fang? Maybe he worships them, like gods or goddesses. Brings them offerings – flowers and bits of bread, like they do in Thailand or somewhere.

Grandpop's parrot was called Viv, after Sir Vivien Richards, the

West Indian batsman. He started to call the bird Sir after Viv
Richards was knighted. Viv was a green and red parrot, very
loving towards Grandpop, but jealous. He was known to give a
nasty nip to anyone Grandpop talked to kindly, so I had to watch
him when I was there. Grandpop usually shut him in the cage
when I was around. Viv and I were in competition. I think
Grandpop quite enjoyed that – these two birds loving him.

I never knew if Viv was male or female. He didn't say much
apart from Hello, and that stupid whistle that means I fancy you.
He died a couple of years before Grandpop and Grandma. Old
age, I think. But they live to be very, very old.

How strange to die of old age. To be so old you just wear out
and fade away.

I think I'm lucky, in a way, to know I'll die young, untarnished
and unwrinkled. Whatever I achieve, people will admire me for
it, because I was young and I died before I could make all those
mistakes ordinary people make. I'll be a hero, sort of. Not like
Beth in *Little Women*, though. You could see she was a victim,
the sickly one with the mark of doom over the door, the sweet,
never did anything wrong, yukky angel. Why does the one who
dies young in novels have to be so bloody goody-goody?

I won't have time to be unfaithful to my husband, or to be a
bad mother, or a failed anything. I have the perfect excuse for
failure – an early death. So I can try anything, do anything I
want, no worries. What do I care about exams? I am the luckiest
person I know. It's just that I have to get in all the stuff I want to
learn now. Now. Before it's too late.

I wonder what happens to all the stuff people know, when
they die. Obviously, if you're a great scientist, or a famous actor,
or a great cricketer, or a great piano playing genius, there would
be a record of your achievements and inventions or discoveries.

Film, video, recordings, books. But what happens to all the little people's knowledge and discoveries? How do we pass it on? How will anyone else know what we did? Does it matter? I suppose writers have found the best way to preserve their learning. If the book gets published, of course. Perhaps everyone should write a book about their life. That way, their grandchildren and great grandchildren will know what they thought about life, and they would pass on their understanding and imagination. I expect we all have at least one insight about something or other that other people might find interesting.

Mum has got lots of herbs growing. Well, a few from car boot sales – basil, ordinary mint and apple mint; oregano, and that very small-leafed stuff – thyme. She would love to grow coriander but it runs to seed, apparently.

I want to get a photo of the badger shoe thief, when it comes again. Maybe I should leave the other shoe out for it as bait. Then follow it and find Mum's other shoe. But I expect it's hidden deep down in a set that goes a mile inland, within an old tin mine. I could follow it into its hole like Alice in Wonderland. Mum's shoes a mile underground… weird.

It won't be the first time Mum has had problems with a shoe fetishist. She always tells this story when anyone admires her shoes: Once, in London, she was driving in heavy traffic and an old bloke put his hand up and stood in front of her car. He was fat, with narrow shoulders and a very fat bottom. He had next to no teeth, and there were long strands of hair pulled over his bald head. And he was wearing a scruffy raincoat. He said she had oil leaking from the engine and should stop round the corner. She did as he said. Yes, she really is that naïve, poor Mum! She parked and he put his head through the car window and saw her beautiful dark red, high-heeled suede boots, and he asked her to put up the bonnet so he could look inside the engine. Being totally ignorant about motors and shoe fetishists, she did as he asked. He then asked her to push her foot down on the accelerator and pump up and down. Then he apparently winked, she said – I think that's what she said – with his hand in his pocket. Oh yes, he suggested that she might like to remove her boots. At this point she realised that something was wrong and gave him a fiver, said thank you, and drove off in a hurry, laughing hysterically. She read in the newspaper soon after, that a man in that area of London had been found with a collection of hundreds of women's shoes in his flat – every cupboard stuffed full of boots and shoes, especially high-heeled shoes. It must have been the same man. Perhaps he died and became our badger in his next life. He was the right shape for a badger, narrow at the head and big at the rear. Pear-shaped. There are some very weird people out there.

CHAPTER TWENTY-TWO

BRETT CALLED FOR me today after breakfast. He just rang the bell. I answered as Mum was, of course, in the bath. And there he was with his floppy hair, his daft curly smile and his binoculars. I was not wearing my hat – a miracle, though obviously I don't care what he thinks, and I stood there like a lemon – how do lemons stand? Like me, obviously – knock-kneed. Actually, I am not knock-kneed. My knees are probably the only part of me that aren't knocked.

I asked him in and gave him orange juice. Mum came out in her dressing gown and with a towel turban covering her wet hair. She was uniquely well-behaved.

Then I went with him onto the coast path and we sat in the same grassy place as before. I didn't say much. He did all the talking. Said he was pissed off coming to England, and I was the first interesting person he'd met. Me, interesting? He's starting at the local school next term. He's twelve next month. He hates skateboarding, surfing and all contact sports. He likes reading – he's told me about a great Australian writer who's written a series of books about these teenagers who have to survive on their own in the Australian bush when the country is invaded (it's set in the future). And says he'll lend them to me.

What's wrong with him? He's too good to be true.

We had a really good time – saw all sorts of sea birds – I was able to tell him what some of them were, as he doesn't know much about English birds. And we looked them all up in my – Mr Writer's – bird books. Didn't see the peregrine again. Brett has a notebook for birds. He wrote down all the birds we saw:

Herring gull – 26.

Greater Black-backed gull – one pair.

Cormorant – 6.

Gannet – 32

Stonechat – a pair.

A possible skylark, but it was too far away to be sure.

I really enjoy being with him.

CHAPTER TWENTY-THREE

Note: A sunny day, so the sliding door onto the deck was wide open and Pop walked in and had a look round. Flo and Rambo were asleep on the sofa – or pretending to be. He wasn't at all concerned when I walked slowly toward him. He casually made his way out the same way he got in. We need another shell curtain.

Last night three badgers came – a large male, a smaller adult and one baby. I put out loads of peanuts for them and chicken bones from our roast supper. They nibbled the chicken bones very carefully, getting every bit of goodness out of them but didn't eat the actual bones. They came just as it got dark so I couldn't take a photo of them as I don't have a flash. I'll never get to take a photo of them. I'll just forget that idea and simply enjoy watching them.

We've freed the racing pigeon. Took it out to the edge of the cliff. It flew.

I HAD A dog once – at least, it wasn't exactly my dog – it was a stray, and I called him Scruffy. He was a sort of rusty red colour with a very waggy tail and a good sharp intelligent head, quite foxy, with yellow eyes and a thick coat. He had a collar but without a name tag on, and I used to tie a belt on to it and take him for walks onto the beach by Grandpop's house. Then I'd let him off the lead and we jumped breakwaters and ran along the edge of the waves and lived in a beach hut. Not really, but pretend. It was lovely. I was so happy. We were free, Scruffy and me.

OK. That whole thing is a lie. It was Mum's story and her stray dog Scruffy. But she's told it to me so many times I sort of think it belongs to me, too. It's part of my story. Mum says her generation was the last to have a 'Free-Range Childhood'. She means that she was able to go out of the garden to play – to run in the fields, climb trees, make dens in places a long way from home. Well, a mile away at least with no adult around to say 'No, you can't do that.' When she was little she would have breakfast and then just get out of the house and only come back at tea time or supper time. Grandma was very strict and even when Mum was seventeen she had to be home by 10pm. But Mum, when she was little, had no fear of anybody kidnapping her or abusing her or anything. She could speak to strangers and nothing awful ever happened to her. When I was small, I used to think that abusing was called abruising – which is a much better word. Kidnapping is a word that means just that – kid stealing – child stealing. So, it's been going on for hundreds of years.

There was an unhappy ending to Scruffy though. Mum was walking to school one day and she saw a dustman pick up a dead dog from the gutter and throw him into the rubbish truck. Yes, it was Scruffy. Mum never did find out who his real owner was.

Grandpop once said to me that I had been given a great gift: the knowledge of my own mortality. He said that most people never really lived at all, even if they survived to be 100. They just let things happen to them and didn't really see the world around them or change anything. He said that I had a unique opportunity to be someone who lived to the full. *Every moment is full of wonder*. He said that. And it is. He's right – was right. He said that I had the privilege of living in a country that had free speech and a free press, and that was the most important thing a government could give its people. *The truth: however unpleasant that might be*. No one here gets tortured for writing poems. That happens in many countries, apparently. Tortured for writing poems? Buggering poodlebums!

He said I should think about producing something to leave behind, or do something to change the world for the better. *Make something beautiful, Princess.*

He said he wasn't capable of creating anything lovely but maybe I would be. What, though?

Mum and I are on our way to Seal Island. I'm so excited. I love little boats. I've been seasick in bigger boats but not something as small as this. We're on the *Island Queen* with lots of holidaymakers. There's a mother with her baby, who has blond curly hair – he's about three. They're sitting next to us in the stern – that's the back of the boat. The waves are bouncing and leaping like frisky lambs, white and fluffy and not threatening at all. It's a perfect day for a boat ride. The baby is trying to catch a wave. He has his plump little arms outstretched and is looking at the wave curled around the sunlight, the pale green glow inside the wave. He wants to take it home. His fingers are trembling. Oh, he's such a darling baby with his blond halo! His Mum is so proud!

An American woman sitting close to us says to Mum, 'Isn't he adorable! When they're babies you could eat them, and when they're teenagers you wish you had.'

Mum – my own mum, that is, looks scrumptious. Her hair has gone very blonde in the sun and she is wearing a lovely floaty white shirt with her jeans. She's lucky in that she doesn't feel the cold. I do, so I've got a heavy sweatshirt on over my birthday T-shirt, and of course I'm wearing my cowboy hat, which keeps trying to blow away, so I have to hang on to it. I don't know what I'd do if I lost my cowboy hat. It's part of my disguise, my persona, my uniform. It's part of Grandpop, and I can't ever let it go.

If I ever get married (which, of course, I won't) my husband will have to love my hat, as well as me. And Charlie too, natch.

The captain of the boat is very old and wrinkled and brown as a conker. He's got a smiley face with smiling lines around his sailor's narrow eyes, and he has faded tattoos like Grandpop's. They must have been bright colours once, when he was young, but now they are like a stained-glass window seen through a fog: pale mauve and baby pink and apple green – anchors and roses and strange fishy creatures.

I do love tattoos. It's like being covered in cartoons; they make me smile, I don't know why. Why do people make patterns over themselves, painting their skin? It seems very primitive, like being a Native American Indian in cowboy movies. An instinctive urge to decorate oneself for something – what? – sex? Like lipstick. (Mum says it's war-paint.) To make your enemies afraid? You must have to be quite brave to put up with the pain of all those needles.

I've had quite a few needles in me over the years. Since day one. I still don't like them and I would never have them for fun or vanity.

I do sometimes think about the dangers and disadvantages of

having a heart–lung transplant operation. But as it's my only chance of a longer life – well, a few years longer, maybe four or five – there's not much choice. I have to go with it. Go for it. Just do it, if I get the chance. Forget the post-op problems – possible tissue and organ rejection, drug side effects. I've no choice. Just go for it. What's there to lose?

The cardiac surgeon has talked me through it and I know what's involved. I think it's rather exciting, actually – like a great adventure. I am a pioneer, going into new territory. Cool. A journey into the unknown. Wowsky! (a Grandpopism I've just remembered). But first they have to find the Holy Grail for me to survive – the perfect match donor. Hopefully, by the time a donor is found for me, I will have completely recuperated from the last operation.

I trust the surgeon – Mr Sami. He did my operation last year, the one that didn't work. He says my particular problem is unique and so there is no known curative surgery. I should have died when I was first born, he reckons. But I didn't. I'm still here. He thought I might have enough pulmonary artery to build on, but I haven't, so that's why the last bit of surgery was aborted or abandoned – he just opened me up, saw what was what and closed me up again. He had hoped to do two operations or even three to make me a nylon or teflon or dacron or whatever artery, but he had to abandon that idea, and just close me up. So now the idea is to wait until they find a donor heart and lungs and give me a completely new set. Well, second-hand.

We're used to second-hand, Mum and me. We're into recycling – the car boot variety.

'Look, a seal! And another, and another!' They're all over these black rocks, lying around as if they are sunbathing. Big ones and little ones. They're wearing their wet suits – black and shiny like surfers – and they have long lovely catty whiskers and black noses and big soft eyes. They look as intelligent as labrador dogs.

It's hardly an island though – just a group of rocks.

The baby is not in the least bit excited. His mum is pointing at the seals and trying to get him to look, but he doesn't care a hoot about them. He takes it for granted that there are creatures around him, a part of the world, as he is. He has no idea that it might be the only and last time he ever sees a seal.

Last times. How do we ever know when it's the last time for anything?

The last time someone says, *Goodnight, God bless.*

That's what my Grandpop used to say to me.

CHAPTER TWENTY-FOUR

GRANDPOP SOMETIMES CALLED me Tiddly Poo. I don't know where that comes from – maybe *Winnie the Pooh*. Tiddly – little. Pooh – bear. So – Little Bear. I always felt safe and very loved when he called me that. Beloved.

Every time I think of him and Grandma not being here any more I feel as if I have been stabbed in the heart, or punched in the stomach. I nearly fall to the ground. Someone said to think of them as if they are in another room. Another room? With a locked door.

I remember Grandma calling me Sweetie-Pie or Sweetheart. My heart is not sweet. It's bloody rotten, actually.

No one really knows why it grew that way – maybe an infection when Mum was first pregnant. I was born with heart failure. My pulmonary artery is only vestigial; which means it's not properly formed. My blood is oxygenated by way of the bronchial arteries, and there are other defects in the heart and circulation too, which actually help the blood get round the system other ways, luckily. So my brain is getting about 75 per cent oxygenated. As it is such a rare condition – babies born with these problems usually die within a few days or weeks – they don't really know what to do with me, or they haven't, so far. They've been making it up as they go along. They admit that. And I'm still here, after all. But now they reckon a transplant might be the answer. A heart–lung transplant.

Last time I went to the hospital I met a boy who's had the transplant. He's eighteen, from London, a terrific athlete, apparently. Marlon. He had become ill very suddenly with a virus that knocks off the muscles surrounding the heart, and had to have an immediate transplant to save his life. He's doing really well, running now, and says he'll keep in touch. 'See you, man,' is what he actually said, but he is eighteen and I am only just twelve, so…

I haven't run since I was… what? Nine? Eight, probably. Who needs to run, anyway?

There is possibly someone just going about their life – eating chips, doing a really difficult maths exam, reading Shakespeare, or listening to a rap record; skipping, washing their hair, playing piano; cuddling their Daddy; writing a poem; just being whoever they were born to be, who will one day soon run out in front of a car, or fall off a bike, or die of some horrible disease, or have a fatal bungie jump. That person – or that person's mother and father – are going to give their heart and lungs to me. What an amazing gift.

My new heart and lungs. A life. A few more years, anyway. Time.

Perhaps I could have had Grandpop's heart and lungs, being as he was closely related. But I suppose they were too worn out by smoking to be of use to a young person; but I like the idea of having his heart beating inside my chest. In a way, I suppose it already is. His genes are part of my make-up. He encouraged me to climb and be adventurous like him, not that I needed to be encouraged.

It was great being with them.

Mum is always – has always been – ultra protective, but Grandpop cheered me on when I did crazy stuff like jumping from roof to roof of the beach huts, and walking along the railings above the beach at Shoeburyness as if I was tightrope walking. I didn't get dizzy in those days. I remember Grandma saying, 'Do you want to kill her?' and Grandpop saying, 'Better she dies doing something she really wants to do rather than dying in bed. Dying in bed is for old people.'

He lives on in my head, Grandpop does, and if I use expressions he used, and if I have picked up his mannerisms, maybe then he'll live on as long as I live – which, of course, might not be long. But maybe whatever I say will be noticed and used in someone else's life, and so my mind, my thoughts, my imagination, his sayings and philosophy, could continue on and on, maybe forever. Maybe. Who knows? We just have to do the best we can while we're here. Otherwise, what's the point?

Poor Rambo is flea-ridden and has an allergy to his fleas. He scratches and has scabs and bald patches. Poor Rambo. Mum grooms all the cats most days. They go to her if she bangs the comb on the outside table. She is quite fierce with them, firmly combing them, head to tail, belly and back, under the chin, on their hard little heads, but they love it. I suppose it's like a really good massage. And she gets rid of some of the fleas. Cat fleas are really hard-skinned – shelled. I find it almost impossible to squash them dead. You have to get them between the backs of two fingernails and press hard until they go pop. And they are so small, they easily escape.

I'm lucky. They don't bite me.

Summer, of course, is allergic. She doesn't come round much – she *didn't* come round much – in the summer holidays, because that's when they are at their worst.

Mum tries to put that stuff on the backs of the cats' necks – to kill the fleas, or make them impotent or infertile or something, but they sense when she is going to do it, and leap off her lap before she can even open the sachet. She's threatening to get the vet in to give them all an injection against fleas.

It costs loads of money for a call out, but it's a lot easier than carrying them all up the hill to the car on her own.

I'm useless when it comes to carrying stuff anywhere, of course. I don't know what I am good for, really. Oh, Buggering Nora! as Grandpop would have said.

Ginnie has been to see me. At last! She rang the doorbell. Mum was at work. I was lounging around in my pyjamas – very embarrassing, but I asked her in for a cup of coffee and while the kettle boiled I got dressed. The cats were all over her. They instinctively know a cat-lover. She asked if I had been watching the peregrine and I said yes. I told her about the badgers and the seals. We went outside and looked through our binoculars at the peregrine nest. No peregrines though. I have arranged to go with Ginnie bird-watching tomorrow at Hayle estuary, if Mum allows me to go. There is a special hut there where birders go to watch all the waders in the river. It's called a hide. She'll pick me up if Mum doesn't want to go. I'll persuade Mum to come, though. I'd like her to come too.

Mum had a good day at work. She's seen a cottage that might be right for us. The right sort of price. She'll take me to see it next Saturday. It's occupied by holidaymakers until changeover day. I'm so excited!

Note: There are two incredibly foreign looking birds on the feeder this evening – red, black and white heads, small, like finches. Goldfinches. They are so exotic they look like they should be in a zoo. Except I don't believe in zoos.

CHAPTER TWENTY-FIVE

SUNDAY MORNING, MUM gave up going to the car boot sale and came bird-watching with Ginnie and me instead. There were all these old people, except for me, and Ginnie, of course. Wrinklies, like Mum, and a few Crumblies. But they were very friendly and welcoming to us. Our GP was there, he was the leader I think, and let me look through his telescope. He had to lower the tripod it was on so I could reach. I pretended I could see what it was we were supposed to be looking at – some unusual wading bird – but I can't honestly say I did see it. That was in the hide. Then we all walked a little way along a footpath, crossed the road and leaned on a wall and looked over towards the estuary. And who was there leaning over the wall with his dad? Brett! His dad is keen on birding too. They joined us as we walked along by the estuary.

I had a good time, and so did Mum, who looked cool in her khaki shirt and camouflage pants. She was wearing red lip-gloss and a khaki baseball cap. (I wore my cowboy hat, of course.) She smiled a lot.

Ginnie is obviously well known to the bird-watchers and knows all about the bird life. She introduced me to everyone, though I can't remember the names.

When she said our name – Stevens – someone asked if we were Cornish, because, apparently, Stevens is a local name. Mum said that Daddy's family was from St Ives. I had no idea. Cool. I might have cousins or something here. Why didn't she tell me before? I need family for goodness sake. I shall look into it.

In the heat of the day the wind's dropped to nothing. No bamboo leaf quivers, no branch of the tall silver tree shivers. It looks like a painting, not alive. The only movement is a spiral of midges: a little cluster of juggled miniature insects in chaotic constant motion, the shimmering cloud staying more or less in one place, hanging above a certain part of the garden in the sun's slanting rays. When I walk along the path where the annoying flock, (that's what it looks like – but not like starlings who all more or less go in the same direction) hangs, my head divides them and they come together behind me. They are in an ecstasy of perpetual motion. Is it a mating dance, an orgy, perpetual emotion? What is their life? How long do they live? Perhaps they are a little treat in the diet of a certain bird or bat. A small amount would have to be very tasty. Like caviar. (Not that I've ever had it, but I've heard about it. Smells fishy, I think. Surgeons' eggs, or something.)

There's never complete silence here, even in the still of this overheated day. The calm sea has dribbled sneakily up the beach and is now racing towards the black cliff, slapping and smacking and spanking the rocks. A hurrying sound. More perpetual motion.

Mum is soaking up the last rays of sun. Her whole body is in the shade except for her face and head. She looks relaxed. The sun wrinkles her blue-grey eyelids and silvers her hair. I can see all the cracks and creases of her skin – especially her neck. It's rippled and crinkled like our beach at low tide. But of course, I say nothing. She prefers to be backlit in public, she tells me. But as it's only me seeing her, she Doesn't Give A Damn. I know where she got that from – poor Scarlett O'Hara! What an absolute turd her husband (or was it her lover) was! Can't remember his name. Ask Mum. Dark, moustache.

Mum says, 'A charming brute, Clark Gable.'

Mum says she wants a bulldog-clip job on her neck and chin, just stretch it all back and tie it under her hair, behind her ears, a ponytail of loose skin. Yuk!

The young herring gulls' voices are breaking. They have a sort of long quivering quaver and their only cry is a simple sound – not complicated speech like the adult gulls have. The adolescents don't chatter or mutter or gossip or complain or laugh raucously. They just yell loudly – *eeeyh, eeeyh, eeeyh*. Like a rusty creaky gate. Like me I suppose, on a bad day.

I had no idea that herring gulls took so much time to mature. They are big like their parents, but naïve and ignorant, lacking the right expression for their feelings. Whatever they are feeling they only have one word for it – *eeeyh*.

I think the adult herring gulls are very intelligent. Pop is anyway. He looks me in the eye. Not many people do that.

Talking of which – Pop has just appeared, as if by magic, silently, on the deck rail next to me. It's tea time of course, and I've fed the cats but not Pop.

He folds his pure white angel wings neatly. They are a pale cloudy grey on top. He has pink legs, with knobbly knees and webbed feet. His left foot is slightly damaged – or the soft web is, or was – but now has mended.

His toenails are black curved claws.

I love his head – he has no eyelashes or eyebrows, but his yellow eyes have an orange line drawn around them – the same orange as the spot on his beak. When a young one wants food he pecks at the orange spot on the beak and the parent regurgitates mashed up food. Pasties, chips, herring, ice cream, whatever. But I have a feeling that Pop is a bachelor. A lonely old widower bird. He does this thing with his legs and wings, he stands on one leg and stretches his other leg and wing out behind him. When he stands side on to me, I can see the hole through his beak at the nostril – I suppose it's his nostril. He is so royal-looking and solitary, just like Jonathan Livingston Seagull.

I wonder if he thinks about me? I wonder if he really is the ghost of my Grandpop?

There are raspberries ripening in the far corner of the garden. They are hidden in a scramble of overgrown pink campion, forget-me-not, white and red valerian, bramble, and another plant, which is tall and pink and hairy. It must be a weed, because it is growing so well. Hemp agrimony. What a wonderful name.

Mum says she wishes she had written down all the silly things I used to say when I was little. Like – we were hurrying through the streets in a rainstorm once, and I said, 'Don't worry Mum, it's only a passing shower.'

And in London Mum had a friend called Isabel. I could never get her name right and called her Bluebell; and I called Grandma's forget-me-nots, do-not-forget-me's.

Aren't little children cool? Perhaps I should have died after I said that.

I'm in bed now and Rambo is snoring next to me. He's dreaming. I know he's dreaming because his ears are twitching, and his whiskers. Is he dreaming of all the mice he nearly caught?

My animals all have their own lives that I know nothing about.
I know very little about anything.

CHAPTER TWENTY-SIX

Note: Those swarms of tiny midges are a sort of crane fly – don't know their name – but I was sort of right, it's a marriage dance: a stag party, males only, dancing above a particular object which they use to take their bearing. Sometimes they choose a clump of coloured flowers, or a brightly coloured plastic bowl. Ours were hovering over the blue chair on the deck. They dance together to attract females. When a female reaches the fringe of the clustering males she is greeted by a male who whisks her off on honeymoon.

'MUM – WHY DIDN'T you tell me Daddy has family in St Ives?'

'I forgot.'

'Forgot? How could you forget something like that? I need family. You're not enough, you know.'

'Gussie, they're your father's relations, not mine.'

'But they're part of my family.'

'Don't bite my head off, Christ! There's only your father's cousins.'

'Well, it's a start. Can't we meet them?'

'No. Yes, I suppose so, if you must. Though I don't suppose they'll be too pleased to see me.'

'Why not?'

'I'm your father's Past, that's why. Not his Now or his Future.'

I am still my father's daughter. I don't say that to her, but I am. I have Cornish blood in me. *Celtic, like the Spanish – passionate. With a drop of black blood in their hearts.*

'When can we see them?'

'I don't know. I can't even remember where they lived. You'll have to wait until your father gets back from wherever he is.'

I look in the local telephone book and there are about three hundred and fifty Stevens in Cornwall, ninety of them in St Ives. Ninety possible relations! I'm going to phone Daddy when he gets back from his trip with The Lovely Eloise.

I've made a birdbath out of an old dustbin lid and dug a shallow hole in the earth to place it in. In the shed I found an old iron rod like a harpoon, with a fish tail on one end and an arrowhead on the other, and stuck that in the ground next to it, and I've hung one of the bird feeders from it, with peanuts in. I'm hoping to attract birds into the garden outside my bedroom window. I expect they'll take a while to get used to it being there. Most of the little birds we see in the garden are outside the dining room where the copper beech tree is. That's because Mum hangs several feeders from its branches and makes sure there's always some sunflower seeds and peanuts for them. We also have a rather ugly but very useful bird table with a pitched roof. Not much bird food goes on that – leftover porridge, rice, apples and stuff for blackbirds – they love apples. You have to cut them in half or anyway open them up so they can smell the sweetness of the flesh.

Rambo, Flo and Charlie have expressed an immediate interest in the birdbath. They probably think it's another water bowl for them, as they have no concept of a human doing something for any another creature. It's all Me Me Me.

The tide has gone out a long way today – that's because the moon is full. It'll be a very high tide later. I don't really understand all that tides and moon stuff.

Mum says she feels the tides pulling her. Does she mean the water is calling to her to have a swim? Or is it hormones? Female stuff. She is Feeling her Age.

Sometimes I come across her in the garden and she's digging or yanking out weeds and her eyes are full of tears.

'It's hay-fever,' she says.

There's often a cat with her when she's crying. They are very sympathetic. I think she's crying about the same things that I'm unhappy about – Daddy leaving, Grandpop and Grandma dying. And her age – she pretends not to care about getting old and being alone (apart from me, that is) but I know she does care.

She's angry with Daddy for going off with a younger woman – well, of course she's angry – but it's not only anger she feels. I think she feels abandoned. And then there's having me to look after. Not even her parents to turn to. It makes me feel guilty, that I'm not strong enough to look after myself, or her.

I suppose I should feel angry with Daddy too. Yes, I suppose I should. I suppose Mum feels as sad as I do about Grandpop and Grandma dying. But your parents are supposed to die before you, aren't they. It's normal and natural. I wish she wouldn't cry. I wish Grandpop and Grandma were here. They'd know what to do.

I remember Grandma's hands – square, red, hardworking hands, the palms lumpy and bony. Her soul was beautiful though. She once said to me, after reading about boys stoning a swan, 'Is there anything more sad than the sight of a dead swan, alone in a field?'

Note: I have just read in the Independent *that snail shells – or any other mollusc shells – can be repaired in a few days. The shell is formed by the mantle, a thin sheet of tissue covering the body of the snail. Specific cells in the mantle produce a matrix that quickly becomes mineralised with calcium carbonate. This is what makes the shell hard. The mantle will continue to secrete matrix until the mollusc and its shell are fully-grown.*

(Matrix – when I was young I thought that was how you spelt mattress. And sandwiches – I thought they were sand witches and I was a bit scared of them.)

You know how often you half step on a snail and break its shell a bit? I have never known whether to step on it harder to put it out of its misery. Now I think I'll leave them to heal themselves.

Inspecting the new bird feeder. Seeds still there, no birds in sight. The creatures all follow me around the garden; even Pop has appeared and stands on the roof looking down on me. Maybe he really is Grandpop come back to watch over me.

The sand dunes on the other side of the bay are bright pink and so are the waves breaking on our beach. Huge numbers of gulls rise from the sea like a shoal of silver fish. It's very peaceful here. Only the sound of the small waves.

Perhaps Mum will find peace of heart here. Not yet, maybe. She's too stressed out, what with me being ill, Dad leaving us, our London house sold, all our belongings in store and we haven't found a home here yet.

That cottage in St Ives we were going to look at next Saturday – it's been sold. I quite like it *here*, actually.

CHAPTER TWENTY-SEVEN

FLO WAKES ME in the night with the sound she makes when she has brought in a mouse. A loud and victorious *Mrow!* I put on the light and find a dead vole. She doesn't like the taste of those, so she doesn't crunch them up and eat them. I thank her very kindly and stroke her head and she purrs with pride. I then pick it up by its tiny pale brown tail and throw it out into the night. No hope of seeing where it's landed. I shall never see a burying beetle at this rate.

I saw the funniest thing the other day in the porch. I saw a mouse eating from the cat plate. Not with the cats there – that would be pushing his luck – but he was helping himself to their leftover wet food. He looked so sweet. When he saw me he ran behind the chest. We also get other people's cats coming in through the cat flap to have midnight feasts. I never see these cats in daylight – only in the dead of night. (The dead of night. Who thought of that expression, I wonder? It's beautiful.)

A ginger tom often comes in. Ginger cats are always toms, apparently.

Grandpop and Grandma's ginger tom was called Tiddles, and Grandpop rescued him from a watery grave – he was a ship's cat's kitten, about to be thrown overboard in a sack with his brothers and sisters. I wonder if the rest drowned? Tiddles was older than Mum, and when he died he was twenty and she was eighteen. She was his pet rather than the other way round, except that he ignored her mostly, she said, and wouldn't let anyone pick him up or stroke him. A loner. I never met him.

What's the point of a cat like that?

'They're allowed to live with people because they let us get comfort from stroking and grooming them.' So Daddy said.

I don't know if I agree. If they are freethinking creatures they should be able to do what they want, like me.

When we first came to this house there were mice everywhere. We didn't know that until this happened: Mum and I had gathered a load of hazelnuts and put them in a lovely big wooden bowl she had brought back from East Africa. She put the bowl under the bed for some strange reason – she was moving stuff around. About a month later she remembered the bowl was under the bed and found it was empty. There were hazelnut shells all over the house – in a wellington boot and in other places but I can't remember where else. And the mice had made a lovely nest inside a duvet – or rather, an eiderdown – in the feathers. They had eaten their way into it, through the pretty flower design. Mum threw it away and bought another. (Car boot, natch.) She'll leave a note for Mr Writer to explain where his eiderdown has gone.

Our cats had a wonderful first couple of weeks hunting. Cat heaven.

The porch-mouse has been here every day, eating the leftovers. Every time he sees me he runs to hide behind the chest. There's a nasty smell coming from the porch, even with the door open. We pull out the chest and find a nest made of bits of chewed up newspaper – well-read mice, anyway – and there's a little hole in the floorboards. Mum throws out the nest, vacuums and scrubs the floor and blocks the hole with a piece of tile. Mr Mouse will find his way out to the garden, I hope. You'd think, with three cats in the house, mice would stay away. But no… cat food is too good to miss. And maybe they like the excitement and danger. Who knows?

I'm sitting on the deck with the cats. They all sit around in quite their own fashion. Flo sits in the smallest possible space. She takes up no room, just her four paws and bottom, tail curled; she sits up straight, watching, always watching.

Rambo is a sloucher. He sprawls with his front legs out straight like a lion and he's getting that square-jawed look that lions have. He has sort of spurs growing on his legs, just above and behind his sooty paws. He's the only one of the cats that positively enjoys having his tummy brushed and stroked. He has got the most beautiful pinky-brown-spotted tummy.

Charlie barely tolerates it and Flo just won't have a hand anywhere near her underneath bits. Her head and back, fine, but no tummy rubs, thank you. Charlie is the most uninhibited of the cats. She lies everywhere, any old how, on her back, on her tummy, on her side. Her coat is particularly thick and soft. I think she would love to peel it off in this hot weather, take it off like a wetsuit. She practically got into the bath with me this morning, lapping at the warm water, tapping my head when I washed my hair. I think she thinks I've taken off my fur (my cowboy hat) when I'm in the bath. Usually, she gets her head between my glasses and the brim of the hat and knocks both off in an ecstasy of love.

My scar is improving. It's very itchy still but it has healed very well. It does look like a shark attack scar.

There are basking sharks here. We haven't seen one yet. They are very big but don't hurt people – they might give you a nasty suck, if you made them cross. They are plankton eaters.

This morning Eugene rang the bell, even though the door was open. Mum thought it might be a recorded delivery letter or an early Jehovah's Witness.

Eugene said, 'There's a parrot in one of your trees.'

He was right. A huge green macaw in a pine tree, looking down at the top deck where we sit and have breakfast. The cats hadn't noticed – I think they must be colour-blind. The pigeons were nowhere to be seen, or the peregrine or the crows.

'He must be from Paradise Park,' said Mum.

Eugene had to finish his round, so couldn't stay to help. Mum phoned Paradise Park and told them about the bird. They had lost a pair of green macaws who had been free-flying the day before. We waited for them to come and get the bird, who was perfectly happy peering down at the banana trees, the tree ferns and bamboos. He must have been flying over the beach, seen the exotic trees and thought he was at home in the tropics.

I talked to him, making a chittering noise with my tongue curled to the roof of my mouth, like Grandpop taught me to do to talk to Viv. The macaw cocked his head and listened to me intently. I wonder what I was saying to him? It must have been interesting, because he kept on listening. I took lots of photographs of him too and phoned the *Times* and *Echo* and told them about the macaw. The reporter is coming straight away. I told him not to bother coming out as I had already shot some pictures he could have, and the Paradise Park people were going to be here in a minute. He said he would come and pick up the film, anyway.

Two men arrived with a large cage and a bag of sunflower

seeds and called to the macaw, but it couldn't fly straight down to the deck, it was too steep a flight path or something, so one of them went into another part of the garden higher up next to the house and called again. The macaw eventually flew across to the hand that held the sunflower seeds and the Paradise man had him. They were delighted to have found him – he was called Harry. Mavis, his mate, was still out there somewhere. Not in our garden, though.

The reporter arrived as they were leaving. He took my film to get it processed and said I would hear from the paper if they used the bird pictures. Later, I was walking round the garden with the cats and I found a tiny perfect bright green feather on the ground under the pine. I have put it in a glass in my room, with other feathers I have found. One of Pop's pure white feathers, a brown female blackbird's, a crow's blue-black feather and a yellowy greenfinch feather.

I had a dizzy spell this afternoon. I'm not good at heights, and when we first came here I couldn't even go out on the deck and look down over the edge at the beach, because it's about forty metres down. But I've got used to it now. I don't know why I felt dizzy. Probably because of looking up for a long time.

When I see Brett I'll tell him about the macaw. He'll be dead impressed.

CHAPTER TWENTY-EIGHT

Note: Two badgers last night – a young one and another. They ate our takeaway fish and chips leftovers. They are coming later every night. Perhaps they've found another good café.

GRANDPOP TOLD ME once about when Grandma fed a hedgehog on their back step, put down a saucer of bread and milk, and in the morning it was still there, and the hedgehog was a scrubbing brush.

A Young Folks Natural History has this bit about hedgehogs:

Everyone knows that the hedgehog is a sworn enemy of reptiles in general and of the viper in particular; but few, perhaps, are aware in what way he contrives to overcome so recalcitrant and dangerous an enemy and make a meal of it. My keeper was going his round – Ferdinand Coste tells the story – this summer in a wood which is unfortunately infested with vipers, when he espied an enormous one asleep in the sun. He was on the point of killing it with a charge of shot when he perceived a hedgehog coming cautiously over the moss and noiselessly approaching the reptile. He then witnessed a curious sight. As soon as the hedgehog was within reach of his prey, he seized it by the tail with his teeth, and as quick as thought rolled himself into a ball. The viper, awakened by the pain, at once turned, and, perceiving his enemy, made a terrific dart at him. The hedgehog did not wince. The viper, infuriated, extends itself, hisses and twists with fearful contortions. In five minutes it is covered in blood, its mouth one huge wound, and it lies exhausted on the ground. A few more starts, then a last convulsive agony, and it expires. When the hedgehog perceived that it was quite dead he let go his hold and quietly unrolled himself. He was just about to begin his meal and devour the reptile when the sight of my keeper, who had approached during the struggle, alarmed him, and he rolled himself up again until the man had retreated into the wood.

That's from *A Young Folks Natural History*. Reading these old-fashioned books written by amateur naturalists is as exciting as watching a good wild-life programme on the telly.

I'm not allowed to say I'm bored. Mum hates it when anyone says they're bored.

Only unintelligent people are bored, she says, and I'm so ignorant I have no excuse to be bored. 'There is So Much More for me to learn.' But nothing interesting or exciting has happened since our bird-watching outing. Can people die from boredom?

There is a thick impenetrable white mist surrounding us. You'd never know where the house is in relation to anywhere else. It's like being in the middle of a pearl. There's no sea or sky or cliff or even garden. We are floating in nothingness, and although it's rather disconcerting, I like it. It's like we're invisible – not of the world, and we can do exactly what we want. It's like being blind. The mist takes away our hearing and sight. But instead of being handicapped, diminished, disabled by our lack of vision, we are somehow more aware of what life is. It's inside our heads, our hearts. All there is, is what's inside of us.

The beautiful terrible world full of earthquakes and murders and miracles out there is obliterated but we remember it vaguely. The mist is a like a wedding veil through which we see whatever we want to see. Our future and our past.

Mum wore a wedding veil. Her hair was long and straight and she wore a sort of tiara of real rosebuds and a long cream silk dress, dreamy and floaty. She looked gorgeous.

I expect she saw her future through the veil and the future was heavenly – life with Daddy. Being loved forever.

And then I arrived on the scene. Mum had some sort of well-paid job in a graphics company, designing book jackets and stuff, but she gave it up before I was born. And since I was born she's not had a job. She's had to look after me. She is doing something now though – Saturdays at the estate agents.

I'm usually perfectly happy to stay on my own for a few hours. I mostly enjoy my own company and if I need her in a hurry I know I can always phone the estate agents' office.

This sea-mist is full of light. I don't know how that is. It's not a grim dark gloomy mist like it was on my birthday, the day of the total eclipse. This is a much more cheerful sort of mist. You can see the water particles, tiny dewdrops, and all the cobwebs on the pines are suddenly visible, glowing diamonds strung on the lacy snares.

I remember a brooch of silver and diamonds that Grandma

wore sometimes that looked just like those cobwebs.

There are two pigeons huddled damp on a horizontal branch, not cooing or moaning. The branches are heavy with moisture, bent low over the deck.

The house is still full of light. Every window has the sea in it. Except today. Instead, it is as if we are afloat in the sea or sky, lost in space and time. Cloudland, where everything is dimly seen. Hazy and filmy, yet dazzling.

It's like being under a mosquito net.

Mum and Daddy and I under a mosquito net together in their bed, laughing as thunder crashes and lightning draws closer all around us, and the flood sweeping red crabs past our wooden house on stilts, and the vervet monkeys screeching on the metal roof.

We have no horizon. Yet the mist is bright. And we are concealed in its blur.

Lost.

I have dreams of being lost. I can't get home. Wherever home might be. There are mountains to climb or broken stairs and ladders, boulders, obstacles on all sides. I miss the last bus/train/plane/boat. The waves are mountainous, the wind furious, the rain torrential. I have lost my clothes, my glasses, my mother and father and grandparents and friends. My cats. Everything. I've lost my way.

Mum and I were on a small tropical island somewhere at night. No lights, not even the moon. We sat on the beach in absolute dark listening to the sound of sand being shovelled until our eyes became accustomed to the night and we began to make out the shape of a huge turtle sweeping away the sand with its flippers and gradually forming a deep hollow. The turtle's eggs were soft white ping-pong balls – a hundred of them dropped into the sand.

We were there for hours, it seemed, and I nearly fell asleep in Mum's arms. And when we walked back along the beach to our room, there was phosphorescence washed in on the beach and I gathered the little balls of strange stuff and wrapped them around my wrist and my fingers like neon jewels – glowing blue opals born in the sea. And then a huge shooting star fell into the sea.

It might sound as if I've made it up, or as if it's a dream, but it was true. It happened. I have a colourful past.

CHAPTER TWENTY-NINE

PARADISE PARK. THERE are aviaries with parrots and other exotic birds screeching and climbing and flying around among foreign looking trees with large leaves. They've all got loads of room and privacy and look very healthy and well cared for. We watch the penguins being fed. Little children throw fresh mackerel to them and the penguins swim and dive for the fish. There's one old man of a penguin, very ruffled and fat, who totters around on the rocks in the middle, and doesn't get anything to eat. Someone throws fish to him, but a herring gull pretending to be a penguin gets there first. I'm sure he'll get fed properly later – the elderly penguin.

We watch the free-flying exhibition. A golden eagle, a snowy white owl, an eagle owl and a bald eagle all fly around and land on various posts or on the handlers gloved hands. It's brilliant. When the birds fly high they are bombed by herring gulls.

There are goats and pigs and ponies and other domestic animals. The goats are from another planet. They have these weird eyes with horizontal rectangular slits as irises. They sort of look at you but they don't have any earthly intelligence. Also, they eat anything, absolutely anything – the paper bag with their food in, and my sleeve, for example. I love the way they kneel on their front knees when they are eating something on the ground.

There's this little girl near me watching the goats.

She turns to me and says, 'Its bottom hole got bigger and bigger and then it did a plop.'

And I say to her, 'That's what your bottom does when you do a plop.' And her eyes get rounder and rounder.

And her mum drags her away to look at the miniature ponies.

My favourite bird in Paradise is a kea. It looks like it's wearing armour. Its beak is long, curved and very sharp. It has an almost human walk, a kind of swagger. The kea stops suddenly and looks over its shoulder at me through the wire. It has a raucous and hilarious cry. I could watch it for hours but we move on as it's lunchtime and Mum's hungry.

'Come on, Gussie, I'm dying for a beer.'

After she's had a beer we go back into the park and have a picnic of egg sandwiches and I feel guilty that we are eating eggs. Stupid, I know. They are organic, free-range, so it's OK.

There's an adventure playground with Tarzan ropes and stuff, which I don't bother with, but it does look fun.

There are even flamingos. It would be great to work here. I love it.

One of the men who had come to our garden actually took us to see the macaws and went inside another aviary to pick up a deep blue feather for me. The macaws look perfectly happy in their leafy home and Harry shows no signs of recognising us. I expect they are pleased to have found each other again, though, Harry and Mavis.

And we feed nectar to the rainbow birds. They perch on your

sleeve and sip the nectar from a little yoghurt pot.

A lovely day but tiring.

We watched *Bringing Up Baby* last night. It's another of my favourite films of all time. Katherine Hepburn and Cary Grant. She is positively anorexic but wears lovely clothes and never stops talking. George, the dog, is a very good actor. He runs off with a precious prehistoric bone and hides it. The best line in the film is spoken by Cary Grant. He says: 'When a man is in the middle of a pond wrestling with a swan he's in no position to run.'

For some reason I thought this was hilariously funny and couldn't stop giggling, and that started Mum off and we nearly wet ourselves, we laughed so much.

'I Can't Give You Anything But Love, Baby.' That's the song they have to keep on singing to Baby – that's the leopard. Except there's another leopard – an escaped-from-the-circus man-eater, and things get complicated after that.

We sat in front of the telly eating our supper – fish soup – which was so delicious I've got the recipe from Mum. I think I ought to get all her interesting recipes. She's ace with leftovers. I'll write them for posterity.

CURRIED GURNARD SOUP
Ingredients:
Sliced raw potatoes
Sliced raw carrots
Rocket
Coriander
3 large tomatoes, quartered
A handful of crabmeat

Leftover curried gurnard from last night

(cooked in green curry paste and coconut milk).

Gurnard is a very cheap local fish, which Mum bought, filleted, in St Ives. She says it is Underrated, Luckily.

Method:
Cook vegetables in stock with tomatoes.
Add rocket and coriander, curried fish, with sauce, and crabmeat.
Serve with croutons – small slices of bread toasted in the oven – and freshly grated Parmesan or Gruyere cheese.

Mum usually makes *rouille*, which is a fiery thick sauce, to put on top of the bread, but the curried fish was hot enough. I suddenly have an appetite for fishy things.

CHAPTER THIRTY

I FOUND THIS in WH Hudson's *The Land's End*:

On yet another morning I was awakened before daylight, but this was a happy occasion, the boats having come in during the small hours laden with the biggest catch of the season. The noise of the birds made me get up and dress in a hurry to go and find out what it was all about. For an hour and a half I stood at the end of the little stone pier watching the cloud and whirlwind of vociferous birds, and should have remained longer but for a singular accident – a little gull tragedy – which brought a sudden end to the feast. The men in fifty boats while occupied in disengaging the fish from the nets were continually throwing the small useless fish away, and these, falling all round in the water, brought down a perpetual rush and rain of gulls from overhead; everywhere they were frantically struggling on the water, while every bird rising with a fish in his beak was instantly swooped down upon and chased by others.

Now one of the excited birds while rushing down by chance struck a rope or spar and fell into the water at the side of a boat, about forty yards from where I was standing. It was a herring gull in mature plumage, and its wing was broken. The bird could not understand this; it made frantic efforts to rise, but the whole force exerted being in one wing merely caused it to spin rapidly round and round. These struggles eventually caused the shattered bone to break through the skin; the blood began to flow and redden the plumage on one side. This was again and again washed off in the succeeding struggle to rise, but every time a pause came the feathers were reddened afresh. At length the poor thing became convinced that it could no longer fly, that it could only swim, and at once ceasing to struggle it swam away from the boats and out towards the open bay. Hardly had it gone a dozen yards from the boat-side where it had fallen before some of the gulls flying near observed it for the first time, and dropping to within three or four yards of the surface hovered over it. Then a strange thing happened. Instantly, as if a shot had been fired to silence them, the uproar in the harbour ceased; the hundreds of gulls fighting on the water rose up simultaneously to join the cloud of birds above, and the whole concourse moved silently away in one direction, forming a dense crowd above the wounded bird. In this formation, suspended at a height of about thirty yards over and moving with him, they travelled slowly out into the middle of the bay.

The silence and stillness in the harbour seemed strange after that tempest of noise and motion, for not a bird had remained behind, nor did one return for at least half an hour; then in small companies they began to straggle back to resume the interrupted feast.

We are gathering samphire from the mudflats in the estuary, close to where the birders have a hide. Not the one we went to, another one. Mum says she and Daddy used to do it when they came here together years ago. Samphire is a fleshy plant, a succulent. You eat it cooked, dipped in hot butter, with lots of black pepper, like asparagus. We have our wellies on. It's a muggy day. The mud is sticky and the samphire is looking brownish as it's late in the season.

'We should have come Sooner,' Mum says.

You snip off the little Christmas-tree-like plants at mud level with scissors. They are about the same height as forget-me-nots. It's difficult to stop once you get into the swing of it, bending like Brent Geese to cut the fleshy stems – you mustn't pull them up by the roots or there'll be none next year. There's a notice saying No Bait Digging. But no notice saying No Samphire Gathering.

There are swans and gulls and lots of LBJ's, (little brown jobs) feeding and grooming and resting in the shallows and on the mud. It's a meeting place for so many different birds. There are good things for them to eat – Lelant lug and ragworm and goodness knows what else. I wish I had my binoculars.

Next time.

We take home two carrier bags full of samphire and have to scrub our smelly muddy wellies as soon as we get there. Then Mum starts to clean the samphire, running fresh cold water through it for ages until all the saltiness has gone, along with any green orange and white ribbon seaweed. Then she strains it in colanders and sticks some of it in the fridge to cook tomorrow.

We have a hot buttery samphire feast tonight, pulling off the steamed flesh from the woody stalks with our teeth and mopping up the buttery peppery juices with thick granary bread. You throw away the stalk and its tiny branches. And tomorrow she'll cook the rest and we'll pickle it with pickling spice for Christmas. She's excited about doing this. She used to pickle onions with Grandma and Wants the Continuity of Preparing Food with me.

'Seriously, Gussie, it's important, stuff like that.'

There are about a hundred and fifty gulls above the house, mostly mature herring gulls but also a few skuas, and our peregrine. At first I didn't notice him, because the gulls are silent, not shouting as they usually do when he is around. Instead, they are united in a feeding frenzy of some flying insect that's just emerged, fledged, and is flying high, and they are sipping the insects from the air, soaring, banking, swerving, and plucking the sweetness of winged insect. It must taste very good. A few juveniles arrive, making lots of squawking racket, but they are no good at it. This is a game of skill.

They better watch and learn.

Pop has deposited – regurgitated, I suppose – several miniscule white crab carcasses on the table on the deck. Their legs are tangled together in a pretty heap, which would make a pleasing brooch if they could be turned into silver or gold. I wish I had kept it to show Mum. Instead I threw it over the deck into our killing fields/cemetery, with the mice, birds, voles, etc. I wonder if burying beetles eat shellfish? I don't suppose they get much chance to try it.

I feel quite exhausted after the samphire-gathering expedition and I'm having an early night with Charlie and a book. It's great here – there are so many books I haven't yet read.

Note: *There is a book-louse, a wingless insect of the sub-order* Corrodentia, *which is found among books and papers. These are small, soft-bodied insects which have an incomplete metamorphosis. As a rule the head is somewhat large, and bears conspicuous eyes (so they can read?) There's also a book-worm – a grub, a beetle larva* (Anobium), *that eats holes in books.*

It would be a wonderful thing to have super-telescopic eyesight so you could see all these tiny critters. Being bionic would be great. Perhaps I could have a leg transplant while I'm at it. Make me taller.

*I can't read this book (*British Insects *by W. Percival Westell) without feeling itchy. There are fleas, flies and parasites for every bird and beast: Bot Flies – Horse Bot Fly, Ox Warble Fly and even a Sheep Nostril Fly. The Horse Bot Fly larvae feed on the lining of the horse's stomach and attach themselves by hooks. As many as a thousand have been found in a horse's stomach.*

*Gad Flies (*Tabanidae*) have lovely names. Blinding Breeze Fly; Rain Breeze Fly; or Cleg; and the Autumnal Breeze Fly. But the Blinding Breeze Fly attacks horses and cattle around the eyes. Clegs are great bloodsuckers and should be studiously avoided. Right, I will studiously avoid them.*

CHAPTER THIRTY-ONE

THE MOST AWFUL thing has happened.

We're having breakfast looking out at a blustery day. The branches of the tall pines are leaning over the house and the palms are clapping. The sea is a boiling white below the house and the tops of the waves are being blown backwards. Crows hurl themselves from the big trees into the wind and don't fly at all, just seem to get thrown about by the gusts, but they seem to enjoy the sensation as they do it again and again.

Pop sits on the rail, his feathers ruffled. I don't know how he keeps so balanced on his spindly legs with his knobbly pink knees.

Mum says, 'Funny, Pop didn't eat his breakfast.'

She had thrown some old bread outside the kitchen door, where he usually waits first thing in the morning.

She starts to clear away and I take my leftover toast, slide open the door and place it on the rail near him. He immediately flies off, trailing a long tail of transparent nylon fishing line from his beak. Why hadn't I seen it before? He had been sitting there for ages waiting for me to help him and I hadn't noticed. Mum and I watch him fly away over the long windblown beach.

'He'll be back, darling, we'll try and catch him and help him then, Don't Worry.'

She's right, he does return. About an hour later, we hear this tremendous kafuffle. He's tried to land on the pitched roof but gets caught up somehow with the line and ends up hanging off the front of the roof, dangling from the line which he had swallowed. It looks like his wing's hurt; he's struggling and fighting the line, like a hooked fish. Just like a hooked fish. Somehow he manages to get back onto the roof and we can see the line's caught on the top of the roof, the ridge. He lies still, exhausted, his eyes closed, facing upwards towards the ridge. He has swallowed the hook and is trapped. His beak is wide open. You can see his black thin pointed tongue.

Mum phones our beach lifeguards to come and help us rescue him, but they don't have anyone on duty. She phones Hayle lifeguards but they can't come to help. She phones the vet, he's closed. She phones the Bird Sanctuary at Mousehole but they can't come out to rescue a hurt bird. But they'll look after it if we take it there. She phones the RSPCA and they said they'll send someone as soon as possible but it might be some time.

I think of Ginnie, find the number, and ring the police station.

'I'll come straight away.' She's so kind.

Pop's still lying there, just keeping still, but every so often opening his eyes and fighting the caught line, jerking his head away from it, making things worse for himself. We find a ladder and put it up at the back of the roof, away from where Pop is, so we don't frighten him more. Mum gets a blanket to throw over him and takes it to the ladder, but she is as bad at heights as I am and can't go up.

Then Pop starts to pull against the line again, obviously in pain. I take the blanket from Mum and climb up the ladder onto the roof and start to crawl towards Pop, clicking my tongue quietly at him. He looks at me and goes quiet. I start to feel dizzy but I don't look down, just keep focused on Pop, and then I hear Grandpop urging me on, like he did when I jumped from roof to roof of the beach huts – *Go on, Princess, you can do it.*

Mum says nothing, just holds the ladder steady.

The RSPCA woman and Ginnie arrive at the same time.

Mum's in tears and keeps saying it's my Grandfather on the roof. They must think we are completely bonkers. Anyway, the RSPCA woman stands on the front deck on a stool, to encourage Pop to move in my direction rather than hers if he tries to get away. Ginnie follows me onto the roof. The gusts of wind are very strong and my cowboy hat is whisked away, taken by the wind and flung over the cliff like a crow. I can't look down. The sea crashing on the rocks below seems very close.

As we edge towards him, Pop starts to sort of swallow more nylon line, moving up towards the roof ridge, and so he frees the line from where it was caught and he flies off, over the sea.

'His wings are all right, then,' says Ginnie.

I don't know how I get down again. I hate heights.

The RSPCA woman says, 'If he comes back, you must try and catch him and take him to a vet to be put down. Gulls die a slow and horrible death with a hook inside them.'

But Ginnie says that she reckons their gullets and guts are so tough, he might survive. The hook might work its way out. She'll come and help catch him if he comes back, if I want her to.

I'm rather tearful, I'm afraid.

Pop is back the next morning, with just a small loop of nylon sticking out from the side of his beak. I give him kitten food from my hand. It's just right for him. He eats it all. He ignores the bread. I don't try to catch him.

He comes back the next day and I feed him again. He eats with delicacy and gentleness, his head on one side, his beak opening just a little to take the mush from my hand. He looks at me. The loop of line is still visible.

We haven't seen him for three days now.

CHAPTER THIRTY-TWO

NO NEWS OR anything from Daddy. Darling Daddy. Why doesn't he love Mum any more? If he can stop loving her, who he promised in church to love forever, he can stop loving me.

No sign of Pop.

I have a cold; I'm in bed. Mum should be at work but she's stayed at home with me. It's not that I need nursing exactly. Just TLC, as she calls it. She brings me hot lemony drinks and refills my hot water bottle when it gets cool. She bathes my pulse points to get my temperature down, the back of my neck, the inside of my wrists and elbows, my forehead. She becomes another person when I'm ill. Not as jokey as she usually is, more serious and concerned, I suppose. She tries not to look worried, but I know she is. She gets these frown lines between her eyes. Very unattractive.

The trouble is, ordinary colds always seem to turn into major chest infections with me, and then it's a long haul back to feeling well again. So she's called the doctor. I've only met him twice: once when we arrived here. Mum took me to see him at the surgery so he could know about me and my situation – I have to have certain drugs, and antibiotics whenever I get an infection. Then on the Sunday morning when we went bird-watching with Ginnie.

Charlie is on my feet. I like having her there but Mum keeps putting her off the bed as I'm getting feverish.

Earlier, Flo brought in a live great tit and Mum rescued it and put it outside and it flew away. All the cats were very excited and searched for it, not quite believing that Mum could have done such a thing. I can't think how Flo could have caught it, unless it was feeding on the new feeder by the birdbath. It is rather low to the ground and maybe Flo was hiding nearby. The birdbath is just outside my room but I haven't the energy to lift myself up and look out the window. Later.

The doctor's very kind. Dr Dobbs. What a friendly name – like an old cart-horse – and he looks a bit like one too – long face, long nose, big teeth, hairy nostrils; didn't notice his ears.

He listened to my back and chest, took my temperature, blood pressure, the usual stuff, admired my shark bite, said it was very impressive, smiled a lot. I like him. He's given Mum a prescription for antibiotics and she's gone to fetch them straight away. Mrs Lorn is coming to sit with me while she's gone.

Mum didn't want to leave me but I'm having a good patch, no fever at the moment, so I'm all right to leave for half an hour. It should have been a locum doctor, as it's Saturday, but Dr Dobbs was at the surgery when Mum phoned and said it was no bother to come on his way home for lunch. Can't imagine a London doctor doing that.

There are two mirrors in my bedroom. The old leather one and another, with no frame. They are opposite each other. I'm frightened to look in either mirror because I see myself going on and on for ever, getting smaller and smaller, as if I am gradually disappearing into infinity or another dimension. It's like that feeling you get when you see a house with a bird table in the front garden that's built to look exactly like the house, and there's a miniature bird table in its front garden, shaped like the tiny house, and there's another bird table... it gives me the williegogs (Grandma's word) just to think about it. Why does it frighten me, I wonder, the idea of something going on and on for ever?

Mrs Lorn is here now. She hums and whistles. Comforting, really, the sound of her somewhere in the house, whistling to herself.

The sea is making too much noise. Booming like a bass drum. My head hurts with the crashing and cracking of waves against the cliff. It sounds like heavy traffic on a motorway. The wind turns into harsh music, like a terrible orchestra playing badly – the conductor gone mad, the music gone wrong. I hate it. I hate it here. I wish we were in London.

I want Daddy to be here, or Grandma, or Grandpop – especially Grandpop.

CHAPTER THIRTY-THREE

Note: *This morning I saw this: A raft of gulls floating in the water together, mostly young herring gulls, and one adult. I looked through the binoculars and saw that they surrounded a dead adult bird, its white breast up, floating. Other birds arrived and settled in the water around the funeral procession. The adult gull stayed always close to the dead bird, his mate, I suppose. They gradually floated out with the tide, always the same few close to the body and others came and went, but there were still about a dozen or more accompanying the body out to sea. There was no noise, no screeching, just a silent procession.*

I'VE BEEN ILL for three and a half weeks, but I'm feeling much better. Weak and woolly still, a bit wobbly, but my chest is clearish. I'm allowed to get up for a couple of hours each morning, if I feel up to it.

It's a lovely warm still autumn day, with white puffy clouds in a perfect blue sky, very Rupert Bear, or even Katherine Mansfield. I'm sitting outside in a sheltered spot, in an old wicker chair, wrapped up in a big fluffy blanket, with Charlie at my feet, a book in my lap, and my binoculars around my neck.

No cowboy hat. It had a burial at sea. Grandpop would have approved. Instead, I have a navy blue England cricket cap with lions embroidered on it. Dr Dobbs gave it to me. He's into cricket.

The other two cats are hanging about, waiting for Mum or me to groom them. We've heard a peregrine and seen it briefly, flying over the house.

And a herring gull stands sentinel on the deck rail, like a guardian angel. Mum said he was there every day when I was ill. Mum says it's Pop. I think it's possibly Pop, but I'm not absolutely certain. He has a little sprinkling of pale brown on his head. Maybe it's son of Pop. He's very quiet and calm, and the cats tolerate him, though Charlie did have a sneaky go at him, reaching up with her front paws when he wasn't looking. But then she ran away, the coward, and hid under my chair.

While I was unwell, Mum has been feeding the little birds even without me reminding her. They have quite taken to my birdbath and the new feeder on the whale harpoon.

Before breakfast – a five-minute egg and granary toast soldiers and fresh-squeezed orange juice – we rescued a live mouse. Flo's, presumably. It had got into the large wooden bowl from Africa that we keep magazines in on the floor. Mum took out nearly all the magazines, so the bowl was light enough to carry outside. The mouse made a great leap for mouse-kind, running up the curved side of the bowl like he was skateboarding and launched himself into the great unknown, over the deck, into the bamboos, with his little legs outstretched, spreadeagled like wings. I think he was OK. The cats don't understand when they've got a mouse in the house one moment, and then it's gone. They carry on sniffing under the furniture for ages, hoping it's still there.

There's a huge circle of brown water near the estuary mouth, like a milky coffee stain on the otherwise pale carpet of green sea. It rained heavily in the night – maybe that's got something to do with it, the sand getting churned up.

The rain woke me and I read for a while and stared at a fly, which was holding the ceiling up. (That's what I used to think they were doing when I was little.)

A daddy-long-legs came in my window and tickled my face and I had to get out of bed to rescue it and put it outside. It's that time of year, apparently, and Mum will have to ask me to pick up large spiders and throw them out. We've got this brilliant spider rescue device that sort of sucks them in when you press the lever and doesn't squash them. They are caught inside a gentle cage of soft bristles until you let them go. She can't even bear having a spider at the end of a long stick, though.

I've missed blackberrying. They were all along the railway line at the end of August and Mum made a blackberry and apple crumble. She says when I'm stronger we can go looking for mushrooms.

There's no one on the beach. Everyone's gone back to school or work. Brett too. He came to see me three times, but I was too sick to see him. He left me the Australian books he talked about. I haven't started them yet. He's left a phone number. I'll see him again.

The mirror of the sea is splintering on the rocks beneath the house.

There's a gathering of young gulls on the beach. A hundred or more herring gulls and a few black-backed gulls standing looking away from the sea towards two or three mature herring gulls, who are in charge. It's a school for gulls. The teachers are telling them stuff – how to chase hawks away, how to behave towards their elders and betters, how to scavenge successfully.

There's no chance of me starting the autumn term at the local school. I have to rest up for a good while longer, get up my strength, so I can be fit enough for a transplant, when a donor is found. I'm on the official list now and have been given a mobile phone thingy – a Life-Call it's called. Daddy says Mum must go and stay with him when I have to go to hospital for the transplant. He's sent me lots of letters and flowers and he's phoned me twice. TLE (The Lovely Eloise) is no more. Done a runner. He's feeling old, he says.

Dr Dobbs comes to see me lots. I think he comes to see Mum too. She loses her frown when he's here and laughs more. He's old – at least forty – but then, she's even older. She's given up her Saturdays at the estate agents. Or they've given her up. He came to supper the other day. We had French onion soup, which is thick and gooey with lots of Gruyere cheese and bread, and I was allowed to pour a little red wine into it, and then we had cranachan because Dr Dobbs is from Scotland.

You roast porridge oats in the Rayburn until they are just going brown.

You melt honey with whisky and stir in the toasted oats.

Let the mixture cool down, stir in double cream.

Let it set in the fridge.

'Heaven in a dish,' Dr Dobbs said.

His name is Alistair and he surfs – even wins prizes.

Mum's dusted the books and put up a new watercolour painting in my room in place of the broken mirror, which she has put in a cupboard. It shows the harbour of St Ives with bright coloured boats and silver gulls sitting on the orange roofs and flying over the little beach.

Ginnie has been to see me several times. She says she has two nieces in St Ives who are Stevens. She'll take me to visit them when I'm stronger.

Mr Lorn brought me a big box of chocolates and Daddy has sent me another bunch of white chrysanthemums. Mummy gave them to Mr Lorn, for Mrs Lorn, because neither of us likes the smell of them. Mrs Lorn has sat with me a couple of times when Mum has had to go out and leave me. She is Cornish too, small and skinny with a sharp nose, like a witch, but she's really kind – brings me little treats – chocolates and biscuits, fairings, she calls them. And she's teaching me to whistle. She can do that really loud whistle where you put your fingers in your mouth – like in American movies when someone in New York calls a cab.

It suddenly occurred to me that Mr and Mrs Lorn would know all about Mr Writer, and be able to tell me what he writes – if he writes. But I haven't asked them. Why haven't I? Perhaps I will one day, but at the moment I want to keep Mr Writer safe in my imagination. Sometimes the truth isn't as interesting as what goes on in your imagination.

Mum's been reading to me lots. I love being read to, it's such a luxury, my favourite treat. Like being a little girl again. It's almost worth being ill for. *King Solomon's Mines* by Rider Haggard – lovely names, both the title and the author. It's a terrific adventure story, like an Indiana Jones movie, and tonight we're watching the old film that was made of it, starring Stewart Grainger, Grandma's heart-throb.

Mum's going to read me *White Fang* next. Jack London wrote it and it's about a dog that's half wolf.

She's fixed it with Mr Writer's agent to stay here another three months.

The best news is, she's found us a house in St Ives through the estate agent she used to work for. She made an offer the first time she saw it. I've got the details in front of me. It's a little Victorian terraced house with a small front garden and views over the harbour and town, like in my new painting, and from the attic room you can see the sun set over Porthmeor. There are families with children living next door each side. She's taking me to see it as soon as I'm strong enough.

We'll be able to get all our stuff from London – all our own books and things, and Grandma and Grandpop's belongings. It sounds almost too good to be true. But Mum says it will really happen this time: she has paid a deposit. I can't wait to go and see it. Mum says I can choose my own room.

I had horrid dreams when I was ill and kept crying out, apparently. Burnt birds, black birds dying horribly, a scalded featherless gull screaming; snow and ice surrounding me, lost – my usual nightmare, with variations. I wrote them down when I was feeling better and that helped me to stop them happening again, I think. My fever has gone now and so have the nightmares.

Last night I dreamed that Grandpop and Grandma were in my room, smiling at me. Both of their cheerful faces above me, smiling. And then I heard Grandpop say clearly, 'Safe journey, Princess. God bless.'

Before dawn the curlews and oyster-catchers were calling to each other as they flew towards the estuary – *I'm here, I'm here,* they called, *don't get lost, this way, this way, this way.*

The Summer Day

Who made the world?
Who made the swan, and the black bear?
Who made the grasshopper?
This grasshopper, I mean –
the one who has flung herself out of the grass,
the one who is eating sugar out of my hand,
who is moving her jaws back and forth instead of up and down –
who is gazing around with her enormous and complicated eyes.
Now she lifts her pale forearms and thoroughly washes her face.
Now she snaps her wings open, and floats away.
I don't know exactly what a prayer is.
I do know how to pay attention, how to fall down
into the grass, how to kneel down in the grass,
how to be idle and blessed, how to stroll through the fields,
which is what I have been doing all day.
Tell me, what else should I have done?
Doesn't everything die at last, and too soon?
Tell me, what is it you plan to do
with your one and precious life?

Mary Oliver

Some other books published by **Luath Press**

Vet in the Country
Russell Lyon
1 84282 067 2 PB £9.99

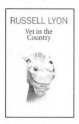

From the Borders of Scotland to the Norfolk Fens, Russell Lyon, author of *The Quest for the Original Horse Whisperers*, shares his lifetime's experiences as a country vet. From midnight call-outs to cows giving birth on the roof, *Vet in the Country* is full of memorable anecdotes and observations drawn from Russell's nearly forty years in the field as a vet in rural Britain.

Describing how his early years on a Scottish farm led to his career in veterinary medicine, Russell uses warmth and humour to share his love of animals and convey to the reader the many trials and tribulations he has experienced as a vet. From his first day on the job being taught how to lasso an oil drum, to his thoughts on current veterinary trends and farming practices, Russell Lyon's *Vet in the Country* is an entertaining and absorbing memoir from an established and respected countryside vet.

A warts-and-all tale of life as a country vet, including amusing anecdotes, dire warnings to those considering entering the profession and nocturnal confessions.
SCOTTISH FIELD

The Blue Moon Book
Anne MacLeod
1 84282 061 3 PB £9.99

Love can leave you breathless, lost for words.

Jess Kavanagh knows. Doesn't know. Nearly twenty four hours after meeting and falling for archaeologist and Pictish expert Michael Hurt she suffers a horrific accident that leaves her with aphasia and amnesia. No words. No memory of love.

Michael travels south, unknowing. It is her estranged partner sports journalist Dan MacKie who is at the bedside when Jess finally regains consciousness. Dan, forced to review their shared past, is disconcerted by Jess's fear of him, by her loss of memory, loss of words.

Will their relationship survive this test? Should it survive? Will Michael find Jess again? In this absorbing contemporary novel, Anne MacLeod interweaves themes of language, love and loss in patterns as intricate, as haunting as the Pictish Stones.

As a challenge to romantic fiction, the novel is a success; and as far as men and women's failure to communicate is concerned, it hits the mark.
SCOTLAND ON SUNDAY

High on drama and pathos, woven through with fine detail.
THE HERALD

Milk Treading

Nick Smith

I 84282 037 0 PB £6.99

Life isn't easy for Julius Kyle, a jaded crime hack with the *Post*. When he wakes up on a sand barge with his head full of grit he knows things have to change. But how fast they'll change he doesn't guess until his best friend Mick jumps to his death off a fifty foot bridge outside the *Post*'s window. Worst of all, he's a cat. That means keeping himself scrupulously clean, defending his territory and battling an addiction to milk. He lives in Bast, a sprawling city of alleyways and claw-shaped towers... join Julius as he prowls deep into the crooked underworld of Bast, contending with political intrigue, territorial disputes and dog-burglars, murder, mystery and mayhem.

This is certainly the only cat-centred political thriller that I've read and it has a weird charm, not to mention considerable humour... AL KENNEDY

A trip into a surreal and richly-realized feline-canine world. ELLEN GALFORD

Milk Treading *is equal parts* Watership Down, Animal Farm *and* The Big Sleep. *A novel of class struggle, political intrigue and good old-fashioned murder and intrigue. And, oh yeah, all the characters are either cats, or dogs.* TOD GOLDBERG, LAS VEGAS MERCURY

Smith writes with wit and energy creating a memorable brood of characters... ALAN RADCLIFFE, THE LIST

The Kitty Killer Cult

Nick Smith

I 84282 039 7 PB £9.99

In the style of Raymond Chandler, this is hard-boiled detective fiction set in the city of Nub; where cats are king, killer and killed. Tiger Straight, PI, is past his prime, homeless and unemployed until the dame Connie Hant shows up. The PI is back, pawing the mean streets of Nub that he knows so well.

Straight has a new mission – to catch the killers of the broad's brothers. It leads him to the murky, tatty underbelly of Nub, throwing up more kitty deaths and a love for a certain make-up artiste. What are the links between these murders and will Straight and his bug loving side-kick Natasha survive to discover the answers before the edible Inspector Bix Mortis?

For those who know and love Smith's first novel, *Milk Treading*, this is the book feline crime hack Julius Kyle started to write.

There's a sense of sheer fun to this world that is more than a little infectious... get in on the act and enjoy a well told tale with a smart sense of humour, a fun plot and perhaps just a little to say about the real world as well. CRIMESCENESCOTLAND.COM

You warm to this dark multi-layered fable that's enlivened greatly by Smith's vivid imagination. THE HERALD

This is a fantastic easy read, funny and smart. SCOTTISH STANDARD

Torch

Lin Anderson

1 84282 042 7 PB £9.99

Arson – probably the easiest crime to commit and the most difficult to solve.
A homeless girl dies in an arson attack on an empty building on Edinburgh's famous Princes Street.

Forensic scientist Rhona MacLeod is called over from Glasgow to help find the arsonist. Severino MacRae, half Scottish, half Italian and all misogynist, has other ideas. As Chief Fire Investigator, this is his baby and he doesn't want help – especially from a woman. Sparks fly when Rhona and Severino meet, but Severino's reluctance to involve Rhona may be more about her safety than his prejudice. As Hogmany approaches, Rhona and Severino play cat and mouse with an arsonist who will stop at nothing to gain his biggest thrill yet. The second novel in the Dr Rhona MacLeod series finds this ill-matched pair's investigation take them deep into Edinburgh's sewers – but who are they up against? As the clock counts down to midnight, will they find out in time?

I just couldn't put it down. It's a real page-turner, a nail-biter – and that marvellous dialogue only a script-writer could produce. The plot, the Edinburgh atmosphere was spot on – hope that Rhona and Severino are to meet again – the sparks really fly there.
ALANNAH KNIGHT

Anderson's brisk, no-nonsense pacing will appeal to fans of crime-writing.
THE SUNDAY HERALD

Me and Ma Gal

Des Dillon

1 84282 054 0 PB £5.99

This sensitive story of boyhood friendship captures the essence of childhood. Dillon explores the themes of lost innocence, fear and death, writing with subtlety and empathy.

Me an Gal showed each other what to do all the time, we were good pals that way an all. We shared everthin. You'd think we would never be parted. If you never had to get married an that I really think that me an Gal'd be pals for ever. That's not to say that we never fought. Man we had some great fights so we did. The two of us could fight just about the same but I was a wee bit better than him on account of ma knowin how to kill people without a gun an all that stuff that I never showed him.

Quite simply, spot on. BIG ISSUE IN SCOTLAND

Reminded me of Twain and Kerouac... a story told with wonderful verve, immediacy and warmth.
EDWIN MORGAN

Ripe with humour and poignant vignettes of boyhood, this is an endearing and distinctive novel.
SCOTLAND ON SUNDAY

Me and Ma Gal was winner of the 2003 World Book Day *We Are What We Read* poll and has been elected as one of *The List*'s 100 Best Scottish Books of All Time.

Selected Stories

Dilys Rose

1 84282 077 X PB £7.99

Selected Stories is a compelling compilation by the award-winning Scottish writer Dilys Rose, selected from her three previous books.

Told from a wide range of perspectives and set in many parts of the world, Rose examines everyday lives on the edge through an unforgettable cast of characters. With subtlety, wit and dark humour, she demonstrates her seemingly effortless command of the short story form at every twist and turn of these deftly poised and finely crafted stories.

Dilys Rose can be compared to Katherine Mansfield in the way she takes hold of life and exposes all its vital elements in a few pages.
TIMES LITERARY SUPPLEMENT

Although Dilys Rose makes writing look effortless, make no mistake, to do so takes talent, skill and effort.
THE HERALD

The true short-story skills of empathy and cool, resonant economy shine through them all. Subtle excellence.
THE SCOTSMAN

Lord of Illusions

Dilys Rose

1 84282 076 1 PB £7.99

Lord of Illusions is the fourth collection of short stories from award-winning Scottish writer Dilys Rose.

Exploring the human condition in all its glory – and all its folly – *Lord of Illusions* treats both with humour and compassion.

Often wry, always thought-provoking, this new collection offers intriguing glimpses into the minds and desires of a diverse cast of characters; from jockey to masseuse, from pornographer to magician, from hesitant transvestite to far-from-home aid worker. Each of these finely crafted stories, with their subtle twists and turns, their changes of mood and tone, demonstrate the versatile appeal of the short story, for which Dilys Rose is deservedly celebrated.

Praise for Rose's other work:

A born professional
MURIEL SPARK

Although Dilys Rose makes writing look effortless, make no mistake, to do so takes talent, skill and effort.
THE HERALD

Rose is at her best – economical, moral and compassionate.
THE GUARDIAN

Details of these and other Luath Press titles are to be found at www.luath.co.uk

Luath Press Limited

committed to publishing well written books worth reading

LUATH PRESS takes its name from Robert Burns, whose little collie Luath (*Gael.*, swift or nimble) tripped up Jean Armour at a wedding and gave him the chance to speak to the woman who was to be his wife and the abiding love of his life. Burns called one of *The Twa Dogs* Luath after Cuchullin's hunting dog in *Ossian's Fingal*. Luath Press was established in 1981 in the heart of Burns country, and is now based a few steps up the road from Burns' first lodgings on Edinburgh's Royal Mile. Luath offers you distinctive writing with a hint of unexpected pleasures.

Most bookshops in the UK, the US, Canada, Australia, New Zealand and parts of Europe, either carry our books in stock or can order them for you. To order direct from us, please send a £sterling cheque, postal order, international money order or your credit card details (number, address of cardholder and expiry date) to us at the address below. Please add post and packing as follows: UK – £1.00 per delivery address; overseas surface mail – £2.50 per delivery address; overseas airmail – £3.50 for the first book to each delivery address, plus £1.00 for each additional book by airmail to the same address. If your order is a gift, we will happily enclose your card or message at no extra charge.

Luath Press Limited
543/2 Castlehill
The Royal Mile
Edinburgh EH1 2ND
Scotland
Telephone: 0131 225 4326 (24 hours)
Fax: 0131 225 4324
email: gavin.macdougall@luath. co.uk
Website: www. luath.co.uk